D0977380

A
Faerie Tale
Romance

K1596

THE DRAGON'S GLARE

"You know what I want." Again, that gaze ran over her, lingering, possessing.

"There are some things even the fierce Dragon cannot have. How pathetic that a man of your stature should be reduced to such bargaining. If I did not find you so deplorable, I could almost pity you."

The hiss of his breath was her only warning before she felt the full force of the dragon's fury. One minute he was relaxed against the desk; the next he was hovering over her, words of righteous wrath spewing from his mouth like flames. "Pity me, revile me, even hate me, but you will only delay what became inevitable the other night. I have no need of bargaining, or even coercion, as you yourself have proved these moments past in my arms. You will come to me soon enough. Not because you have to—*because you want to.*"

COLLEEN SHANNON

The Gentle Beast

LOVE SPELL **NEW YORK CITY**

LOVE SPELL®

October 1996

Published by

Dorchester Publishing Co., Inc.
276 Fifth Avenue
New York, NY 10001

The name "Love Spell" and its logo are trademarks of Dorchester Publishing Co., Inc.

Printed in the United States of America.

THE LOVING SYMBOL
by Colleen Shannon

Years come, years go.
Everlasting love remains,
Lovely seeds to sow,
Legacy the child retains.
Opulent family fable shows:
Weds the Beauty, joy attains.

Rubies, diamonds, pearls of light,
Our heritage be, from Kimball to Kimball.
Sad made glad by Beast of Night,
Eternal, loving fairy tale symbol.

The Gentle Beast

Chapter One

On Callista Raleigh's last night in the only home she'd
ever known, she awoke to find her nightmares reality:
he had come.

At first she discounted her unease. It was her wont,
this past year, to awake with pounding heart and dry
mouth, suffering again that dread that had no name
and no face.

She sat upright, clutching the covers. "Who is there?"

Silence. She peered into the gloom, her breath frost-
ing in the icy air. She shifted her hips on the hard-
packed feather mattress. This month past, there had
been no servants to fluff mattresses or even to cook.
She was alone in the house with her ailing stepfather
and drunken half brother. However, Cerberus, her
mastiff, guarded the entry. She listened intently, but
he wasn't barking.

What had awakened her?

Wind whistled through rotten casements and

9

groaned down empty corridors. Tomorrow their very beds would be sold; no wonder her nerves were on edge.

Still, her gaze returned to the fraying draperies tossing like lost souls in the darkness. A man could easily hide in them. Did this . . . beast lurk there, preparing to exact his ultimate revenge?

"Nonsense! No more gothic novels for you, my girl." The sound of her own voice reassured Callista.

Another loose roof tile or window shutter had rattled. She pulled the covers to her nose and shut her eyes. She needed her rest for their move to the tenant cottage the next day—a move she would have to manage. She was good at managing, she thought bitterly. She'd learned to do so the hard way while the unentailed estate that had been in her mother's family for ten generations fell to rack and ruin.

Her former estate, she corrected herself grimly. Lurid images of dragons spitting fire and knights wielding flaming swords fought endless battles in her mind.

If only she could face their tormentor. Surely the beast ravaging her sleep and sanity would turn out to be only a man, once he revealed himself at last. But her stepfather refused to share his suspicions of who their enemy was.

However, he could not deny the fear in his eyes. . . .

Only this evening they'd argued about it. "Callista," he'd warned in the bare study, "he hates me too much to watch me suffer from afar. He will come. Soon. Almost, I look forward to meeting him."

Callista had admired her own control as she calmly set her stepfather's tray on a packing crate. She'd made the soup from the last vegetables and the bones of the hen a kindly tenant had given them. She'd stretched the scrawny chicken into meals for a week. Now even the bones were boiled dry.

She neatly aligned the wooden spoon beside the chipped bowl. "Perhaps I could heed your warnings better if you supplied me a name."

Henry Albert Stanton, Earl of Swanlea, shoved the tray away. The crate wobbled; the tray clattered to the floor. Soup splatters made a starburst pattern on the marble, washing enough of the grit away to hint of its once fine quality. "I cannot drink this swill. Not fit for swine, much less nobility."

She glared at him.

He leaned his head back wearily. "The only man who could hate me enough to do this is dead. Or so 'tis said."

"I am two and twenty, past the age for coddling. Who was—or is—this man?"

He turned away to gaze broodingly into the fire. His powdered and peruked head sat arrogantly on his stooped shoulders. The famed Yellow Rose, set in a stickpin, glittered at his throat. The priceless canary yellow diamond in a double rose cut was as big as a prune. He'd never sell it, no matter if their ribs caved in.

How could she blame him? She knew he'd treasured the stone from the time when, as a young man, he'd brought it back from India. It was far more precious than the thousands of pounds it would yield at auction, despite the ugly secrets surrounding its acquisition.

She looked at the emerald on her finger and thought of her racehorse, Paris. She couldn't bear to sell him. Not yet. They had a place to live, at least. But how could she help her family out of this devilish fix if her stepfather insisted on protecting her?

Pleas had availed her nothing, so she held her tongue. Attacking one another would serve *his* purpose, not theirs. She knelt and picked up the broken crockery and wooden spoon.

Her stepfather brought his open palm down on the empty crate, making it screech against the floor. "Damn his miserable soul to hell! Somehow he will pay for this."

Callista stacked the dishes back on the tray. "I should think you would tire of vengeance. The trouble with asking for one's pound of flesh is that only bones are left behind, not satisfaction."

The earl followed her gaze to the pot, where white chicken bones had floated to the top. "Curse him, that's all he intends to leave us—bones."

Sighing, Callista returned to her own soup and forced herself to pick up her spoon. One member of this family had to be practical. As usual, it was she. "What have you done to make someone hate you enough to ruin you systematically with the company?" She sipped daintily.

"I do not know, I tell you," he blustered. "Water under the bridge anyway. Besides, the British East India Company has little use for old employees. Once I was too ill to rule those blasted heathens, my time was numbered."

"Your fortune was not. Nor was my own." Callista bit her lip, regretting the retort. He'd not squandered their money; it had been spirited away by a man as evil as his influence.

A patrician white hand squeezed the lap robe. "Anyone can pick bad investments. Especially when they're so tantalizing."

Callista took her last sip. "As you say, it is water under the bridge. Our only remaining decision is simple: what do we do now?"

The Gentle Beast

Henry checked his pocket watch. "Damn the boy, where is he?"

Callista stiffened. "You surely will not agree to Simon's idiotic notion!"

"If we can raise the money, this may do the trick. Eventually. I've never seen anyone with a better head for cards than you. With your looks, you'll draw every man in London to our tables."

Callista straightened martially, then picked up the tray and held it before her like a shield. "I shall not be associated with a gaming hell, even if you can raise the capital. I certainly shall not sell Paris to aid you in such a scandalous cause. My mother would turn over in her grave to see me in such a place."

"Survival is hardly a 'scandalous cause,'" he retorted. "How do you think your mother would feel to see us living in a hovel, off the spurious largesse of the man who destroyed us? Damn his impudence, inviting us to live like peasants in one of our own tenant cottages! I shall see him in hell first!" His large dark eyes glowed like charcoal from ashen folds of flesh.

Callista surveyed him sadly. Illness and worry had stolen the good looks he'd passed to Simon. His bold nose resembled a beak now rather than a Roman coin. His high cheekbones and full lower lip were all that remained of the Greek god who had turned her mother's head away from her fiance, Bryant Kimball.

Unable to stomach the endless argument, Callista carried the tray back to the kitchen, searching again her scanty knowledge of the past for a clue to the quandary of her present. The Kimball match was encouraged by the Raleighs, for Bryant Kimball was a widower with a son; the motherless boy and the fatherless Callista would gain the parent each lacked. Callista's mother Mary was not opposed to the match because she never expected to love anyone as much as Callista's father, her first reckless young husband who had died as he drove the mail coach along the Dover road in an attempt to win a bet.

A gambling predilection, Callista realized grimly, that she shared . . .

However, when Kimball introduced his fiancee to Henry, his best friend from their joint service in the East India Company, life—and love—stirred again in her heart. Clandestinely, Mary and Henry wed. Kimball vowed to ruin Henry. Taking his ten-year-old son with him, he rejoined the British East India Company, only to die in a pirate attack. Rumors abounded that the attack was planned by a company rival, but no proof was ever found.

A cousin had related the old scandal to Callista. She had never believed that her stepfather, who had been a loving husband and father, was capable of planning the attack, as some whispered.

Yet now, alone in the dark, the question returned: if Kimball were dead, who was their implacable enemy?

Creeeak . . . Callista bolted upright.

That noise came from the inside!

She tossed back her covers. Her stepfather had been awakened by the storm and was probably struggling downstairs for more firewood. That was all. Naught to be concerned about.

Callista lit the candle beside her bed. Maybe now, in the dark of night, he'd supply the answers he'd denied earlier. If Henry's misbegotten youth had ruined their future, she had a right to know why. The dread in his eyes proved he at least suspected their tormentor's identity.

She slid her feet into her slippers, throwing her robe on carelessly. The circle of light was feeble, and as she opened her door, the flame guttered. She paused, cupping it with her hand until it brightened again. Of necessity the long trek down the hall was slow. She started with every creak of the aged plank floors.

She'd only heard the old house settling, she tried to tell herself.

"No—" The one muffled word stopped Callista in her tracks. That was Henry's voice. Weak and choked off. Dear God, was she too late?

She leaped the last few steps to the door, unaware that her heavy robe came open. The knob felt icy under her shaking fingers, and she struggled to twist it. Flinging the door wide, she hurried inside and held the candle high; the gale from the open window snuffed it instantly. However, the lantern beside the bed cast a luminous glow.

The magical golden circle was too weak to charm the darkness. Her nightmares appeared incarnate before her. The candle fell from her limp hand.

Someone—something—hovered over her stepfather, a misshapen hand covering Henry's mouth. She saw a hunched back clothed in black velvet, heard a deep voice threaten, "Oh no, my dear Henry, I shall not kill you. That is too quick, too merciful. Your suffering has only begun. You will live as I lived, thankful for your squalor . . . dine as I dined, fighting rats for scraps. . . ."

The vitriol was made all the more caustic by that deep, calm tone. Too late, Callista covered her horrified gasp. Instinctively she backed away, thinking to fetch Cerberus, but the wind caught the door and banged it shut.

That humped back straightened. The heavy velvet cape settled about strong, boot-clad legs, revealing a sword-straight spine that slowly turned. Callista scrabbled behind her with one hand for the knob, fearing that if that Medusan gaze touched her she'd turn to stone on the spot.

She might have escaped had her stepfather not sat up as soon as the hand released his mouth and cried, "Run, Callista!"

The knob turned. She began to pull the door open, but her eyes, mesmerized, leaped upward. She choked back another scream, faltering.

His sibilant whisper took her name and twisted it. "Ah, Callisssta . . ."

In one bound, the beast, for she could name what faced her naught else, was on her. His huge right paw slammed the portal closed and rested there beside her head.

She tried to grow into the chilly wood at her back, but for every centimeter she retreated, he moved closer. Soon his immense chest pressed against her. His warmth might have been soothing in other circumstances, but as it was, she realized only that her robe had come open and that this . . . entity was more monster than man. She felt the silk shirt rubbing against the vee in her neckline; beneath the silk, she felt muscles as steely and resilient as well-oiled springs.

The one glance at his masked face had terrified her, so she concentrated on the patch of black hair bristling between the lapels of his shirt. The hood of his cloak covered his head, so she couldn't see his hair, but her imagination ran rampant. Had the very night come alive and sent a werewolf to kill them?

"Let me look at you." A specially made leather glove covered the three middle fingers of his left hand. He had no thumb or little finger, and Callista's skin crawled at the contact as he forced her chin up.

He moved slightly aside. Callista blinked as blessed

light fought his spell, but the apparition did not disintegrate, as she vaguely hoped. She swallowed, forcing down her panic.

Once, alone in the woods behind the estate, she'd faced a hungry wolf. She still remembered its bared fangs, the deep-chested growl. Some instinct had warned her not to run. Instead, she'd stared into the wolf's glowing eyes, then rushed forward, making her cape flap in the breeze, waved her arms, and screamed as loud as she could. The wolf had bolted.

Only similar tactics could save her now.

The mask was not as terrifying on second glance. But no mere wolf looked back at her. This predator was solitary, mystical, legendary in strength and fierceness. The leather had been sewn into the eternal grimace of a dragon, giving no hint of the true form beneath. The snout was pulled back into a roar and a hole gaped where the mouth was, revealing perfectly shaped masculine lips. Stylistic horns grew out of the wrinkled forehead. The eye slits were slanted, allowing only a glimpse of a pale glitter as those eyes, in turn, examined her.

Her fingers curled against the door. Any moment she expected fire to singe her end to end, but her initial shock had faded as her iron will recovered. She stood tall, her mouth firm, her chin high. He'd taken enough from her. Be damned if he'd purloin her self-respect as well.

Mettle was taken and measured; a battle plan was calculated in two opposing minds and two proud hearts.

Appropriate, Callista thought, that the dying English winter writhed outside. Death and decay surrounded them.

Winter presages spring, came the rogue thought. She

Colleen Shannon

quelled it and calculated her best move. The acuteness of his attention was all too familiar to her, and dread settled in her stomach. For the thousandth time she wished God had not blessed her so richly.

This time, however, her appearance served her well. He would not expect her to be smart enough, or brave enough, to defeat him. She looked like a nymph who should be cavorting on a Grecian urn, as so many men had told her. She sent her stepfather one glance, flicking her eyes toward the poker at the fireplace. She only hoped he was strong enough. He nodded imperceptibly and began to inch out of bed.

Callista looked straight into those shadowy eye pits. "Who are you and what gives you the right to disturb our rest?"

That powerful frame vibrated with mocking laughter that made their torsos rub intimately together. This time she didn't bother to shrink away, but she wished she'd taken time to tie her robe tightly.

"Your first lesson you shall learn this very eve: I do not ask for rights. I grant them." The three-fingered hand drifted down her throat, dangerously close to the vee of her bodice. His gaze tracked his hand.

She sighed her relief when he moved farther away, the better to see her. She suffered his appraisal to give her stepfather time. Almost there. She bit her lip as metal scraped against stone when Henry lifted the poker, but the dragon was too intent on his visual ravishment to notice.

She was tall and willowy, her tiny waist and delicate bone structure giving the impression of fragility. But her dainty hands had a bruising rider's strength; her exquisite face was modeled with the purity only character grants. Her thick hair, spilling to her waist like angel light, cast an aura of gold and red, every strand

18

The Gentle Beast

reflecting myriad hues. Her fearless eyes belied the quivering in her knees. The almond-shaped windows to her soul were an unusual shade of green, the color of a sunlit pond or tender seedlings. They reminded men of spring and its eternal rites. Curling dark lashes framed them, and her dark brows made perfect arcs above them. Her skin was cream rather than ivory. Exactly five freckles dotted her perfect nose.

Broad shoulders lifted in a contented sigh. "Callista. Greek for *most beautiful.* Your mother named you well, but then, you have much the look of her." Almost tenderly, he brushed back a thick lock of hair from her cheek, turning it this way and that to admire the play of red and gold.

Her bravado weakened as he confirmed her greatest fears. She snatched her hair away. "Who are you? How do you know my mother?"

"You may call me Drake."

Of course. What other name would a dragon take? Keep him talking. Her stepfather was only five steps away now, his bare feet soundless on the boards. "I'd lay odds that is not your real name."

"Ah yes, I have heard that about you. For a woman, you are supposed to be quite good at cards. I shall test you. Soon."

That shadowy gaze enveloped the rich bosom her thin night rail hinted at. Callista bit her lip on the urge to tie her robe. Two steps away. She blurted, "I never lose."

"*Never* is a futile concept only Westerners hold dear. As for losing, it is the fires of suffering and loss that forge character." He reached out casually, without turning his head, and backhanded her stepfather. "I shall be the making of you, my dear Henry."

Henry fell, the poker clattering to the wood floor.

"You fiend!" Callista shoved his powerful frame away, dimly aware that she could do so only because Drake allowed it, and helped Henry up. Arm in arm with her stepfather, she spat, "Get out. You've had your pound of flesh. I pray you choke on it."

"Quite the contrary. It tastes wonderful." Strong white teeth snapped together several times.

Her eyes widened, and she couldn't control the shiver that ran through her. Her hand drifted to her throat. She could almost feel those teeth squeezing there.

Henry stood as tall as his stooped spine would allow. "I am not without friends, you bastard. You shan't persecute us without retaliation."

"Good. You'll make better prey, my dear Henry."

Sheer fury drove Callista's fear away. She took an angry step forward. "If it is a fight you want, a battle royal you shall have! My name is Raleigh, after all."

Henry tried to pull her back, whispering desperately in her ear, "No. This is exactly what I wanted to avoid."

She didn't even hear him.

That wide chest shook again. "Listen to the little pigeon." His teeth snapped together. "Hmm, I can't wait to see how tender and tasty you are."

His mockery literally made Callista see red. She was tempted to reach for the poker, but his casual stance, arms crossed over that immense torso, didn't fool her. The unexpected. That was the trick with such as he. Sticking two fingers in her mouth, she gave a long, shrill whistle.

A deep, baying bark answered. A heavy weight pounded up the stairs.

Drake's arms fell, but he didn't bother to lock the door, as she expected. His deep bow had surprising grace for one so large. "I can be polite when it suits me.

The Gentle Beast

This is your home, milady. For one more night."

Callista flinched when he strolled toward them, but he only passed on his way to the window. Callista stared. There was no balcony, and they were three floors up. Cerberus was tromping up the corridor now. She whistled again to guide him.

Drake sat on the broad sill and paused for a last glittering inspection. "For your own sakes, learn, both of you, that my life has depended upon my intelligence. You shall soon discover that danger has a certain liberating quality. Nothing is more conducive to risk than realizing one has naught to lose."

Cerberus burst through the doorway, eleven stone of protective fury. He paused, sniffing the air, then growled, baring his formidable fangs. His black ruff stood on end and his ugly mastiff face fixed into an even uglier snarl.

"Get him, boy!" Callista cried.

Cerberus bounded forward, his muscles rippling in the lantern light.

Drake swiveled lithely and dissolved into the night.

Callista and Henry stared at one another. They hurried to the window. Drake seemed suspended on the side of the building like a bat. Callista's skin crawled until she glimpsed a rope twisting below him. When his boots touched the ground, he looked up at her. He blended too well with the night for her to see much, but his strong white teeth gleamed just before he blew her a kiss.

Swallowing a frustrated groan, she slammed the window down, narrowly missing Henry's fingers. "He shall pay for this."

Henry collapsed on the side of the bed. "Tsk, tsk. Do you want your own pound of flesh now?"

She glared at him, then blew a breath through her

21

lips. "I did sound rather like a prig, did I not? But I confess I now see your point. We shall open the gaming hell, regain our fortune, and wish him to the devil he so resembles. Why should he be allowed to persecute us with impunity?"

Her stepfather lay back and drew his covers up, folding his hands contentedly over his chest. "That's my girl."

Callista's hair glittered about her like a ruby-and-gold-encrusted cape as she strode up and down, ruminating aloud, "The trick is to find his weakness. I saw little evidence of any tonight, but he must have at least one. I shall uncover it."

"Do not trouble yourself. When I found his name on the documents holding my notes, I found out all I could, which was little."

Callista pivoted. "And what, pray, of your claim of uncertainty as to our enemy?"

"I said I suspected. I also said I wanted to keep you safe. I never wanted you to meet him. What would you have done had I told you that Drake Herrick, sole owner of Herrick Importers, Ltd., was the man I suspected of hating me?"

She caught her breath. The name was bouncing around London like a wayward cricket ball. Herrick had appeared in London about a year ago—coincidentally, about the time their debts began being purchased anonymously and their latest investments began going sour.

Much was whispered about Herrick but little was known other than the fact that he'd returned from adventures in the East rich as a nabob and was believed to be English by birth. He'd proceeded to buy London's best hotel and had purchased a seat on the new stock exchange. He was also rumored to have varied interests, ranging from commerce to finance to mining.

This was the man who hated them? Dread dried her mouth, but her reckless streak came to the fore. She smiled, exhilaration giving her a glow that was brightest, though she did not know it, when her cards were poor and her bet high. "I would have gone to London immediately to face him, of course."

"Precisely."

"What, then, did you discover?"

"Precious little. His employees are mum. They refused the bribes they were offered. I suspect fear motivates them rather than loyalty. His business associates know little of him save that he's ruthless when crossed and has the best business instincts they have ever seen. No one even knows where he lives, much less anything of his family."

"He is not married and I very much doubt that he has any living family."

Henry arched a curious eyebrow. "How in the deuce do you know that?"

"Because feminine instinct, if you will, warns he is as solitary as a tomcat and just about as kind. He obviously knows nothing of love or gentleness or even, I suspect, of happiness." Her voice had softened and she couldn't squelch a dart of pity, even though she found the feeling ludicrous.

Henry blinked in alarm. "Now see here. This man is not one of your wounded chicks or motherless kittens. He is dangerous. He has taken our material possessions, but you, at least, still have something of value. For all I know he may even be the sort of man who . . ." He coughed delicately.

She shrugged, her hair rippling with life at the movement. "He does not frighten me." *Not much, anyway.*

"He should. And if you do not stay strictly away from him, I predict he shall."

"What do you plan to do?"

"Be as meek as he obviously expects. I shall move into his cursed hut and live off his cursed generosity. As long as it suits me. Until we raise the funds. Then, if he loves to game as much as is rumored, we may have a chance to win everything back." Henry crossed his arms behind his head. "How fortuitous his visit was. If he only knew how much trouble he has saved me." Henry smiled.

She loved Henry, but she wasn't blind to his flaws. He'd learned the skill of manipulation in India, where it was an art. She looked him square in the eyes. "I support you fully now. I'll even consider helping you in your, er, new enterprise, but no amount of coaxing will make me agree to sell Paris. He's the last remnant I have of Mother. I mean to keep him."

Before the trouble had started a year ago, she'd used the trust fund she'd come into on her majority to fulfill her lifelong dream of owning a horse that could defeat the famous Eclipse. What horse had a better chance than one from the same stables?

When Paris had been offered for sale, his price as Eclipse's brother had been shockingly dear. But she'd run her hands over his hindquarters and fetlocks and agreed to the larceny. She'd had ten pounds left in her fund when the bill was paid, but twenty years of joy to come for it and, if he won the races she hoped he would, he'd recoup his cost many times over in purses and stud fees.

Her stepfather's hand squeezed her shoulder. "If you will not sell Paris, at least consider Quartermain's suit. With a little encouragement, he will make you an offer. His father would love to have a Raleigh as a daughter-in-law. Be careful you do not end on the shelf, my girl. At two and twenty you are teetering on the edge."

Callista disguised her shiver by pulling away to clasp her elbows. "Better than falling off it into God knows what fate by wedding that awful man. Why, *you* do not even like him."

"He would not have been my first choice for you, I admit. But since young Heath died . . ." He trailed off, apparently aware of her tension, and concluded, "If you cannot love again, you might as well ally yourself with someone who can do us some good."

Familiar pain seared her at the name she seldom allowed herself to think of, much less speak. "Don't."

That long hand clasped her shoulder again. After a moment he said lightly, "Perhaps Paris will win us a fortune. Wouldn't that be something to see—him beating Eclipse."

Grief dissipated under the pleasant dream that had kept her going the past year. Its reality, however, now seemed farther away than ever. It took money to enter and train a horse in the most prestigious races. But how lovely it would be to see Paris defeat the unbeatable stallion.

To achieve that goal, she realized distastefully, another would have to fall by the wayside. *Forgive me, Mother.* "Perhaps if you offered to make Quartermain a third-share partner in the gaming hell—"

"He'd be mad to take a third and put up all the funds. No, our only hope of making a go of this is to raise at least part of the ready ourselves. The question is, how? We have sold everything of value that we can and still cannot meet the debts."

The Yellow Rose glittered atop the dressing table across the room, but Callista avoided looking at it as studiously as Henry. Perhaps there was another way.

"I will challenge Herrick to a game."

Henry clenched her hand hard. "Nonsense. You've nothing of value to put up for stakes, anyway. Nothing you can spare."

"I have Paris."

He sat up. "You fickle chit. Why on earth would you refuse to sell him, when we'd at least be assured of a good price for him, and then risk him on a game you could well lose?"

"You know how good I am at piquet. I don't mean to lose."

"Neither did I when I invested our last pounds in that infernal new machinery that turned out to be useless. I forbid it. You shall not go near Herrick."

She fluffed his pillow. "We will talk more tomorrow. We both need rest. Good night, Henry." She kissed his crinkled brow.

Brooding dark eyes watched her on her way to the door. "That missish face will not work. I will have your obedience on this, girl."

"Good night, Henry," Callista repeated, opening the door. She smiled at his muffled curse, her spring green eyes alive with burgeoning anticipation.

Eventually sleep came, only to be routed by the dawn in a few short hours. Heavy eyed, she rose and saw that the farm lad had fetched the few personal possessions they'd salvaged. She'd even sold some of her more expensive gowns. When all was loaded, Henry and Simon rode in the cart. She walked slowly to the decrepit stable, regret and torment dogging her every step.

The Raleigh summer house was unique among English nobility in its line of bequeathal. An eccentric female ancestor of Callista's who had inherited the estate from her father had never wed. Her will stipulated that the estate could remain in Raleigh hands only on the distaff side of the family and only if the eldest female retained the Raleigh name even upon her marriage. Male relatives were scandalized. One disgruntled elder brother even fought the will in court, but the estate was unentailed and the court found the woman of sound mind.

Callista was the fifth Raleigh woman to inherit. Curiously, despite wheedling and bullying from successive male relatives and spouses, the Raleigh women persisted in codifying the original will in their own bequeathals. Having run the estate since her mother's death, Callista shared their determination in full measure.

Quite simply, it was liberating to be sole owner of a vast estate. Women were supposed to be meek and helpless, but the skills required in estate management were exactly the opposite. From an early age, Callista had learned scandalous things for a young woman: mathematics, history, the classics, literature, fencing, horse breeding, chess, and even, from her stepfather, cards.

That unusual legacy would now end. Callista could feel her eccentric ancestor glaring at her from the beyond. But what was she supposed to do? Let her stepfather go to debtor's prison? She'd trusted him with her own funds, since he had, after all, replenished his depleted family fortune with the British East India Company. His investments had always proven solid and she'd wanted to devote her time to readying Paris for his first race.

She opened the stall door and rested her head against the sleek side of her most cherished possession. "Oh, Paris," she whispered, "what am I to do?"

She bit her lip to stifle the tears and drew back to

look at him. He was a deep-chested, tall bay with black stockings on all four fetlocks and a black mane and tail that emphasized his stunning mahogany sheen. He had the distinctive, long thoroughbred legs and arched neck. Every inch of him, from muzzle to tail, was built for speed and power. His perfectly formed head, ears erect and dark eyes alert, turned. He snuffed at her hair, as if wondering at her tears.

His warm breath tickled her ear. She laughed and stroked his velvet nose. He was the joy of her existence. He never scolded her, he never came in drunk, he never demanded anything but oats and an occasional lump of sugar. But he ran his valiant heart out for her. With that curious sensitivity of animals, he was even trying to comfort her.

"You are right, as usual. My own carelessness got me into this coil and only I can get myself out. Come on, boy, it is time to begin our new life." She attached the worn sidesaddle and mounted.

As they rounded the curve leading to the drive, she stopped for one last look. The mellow stone had aged as gracefully as the architecture. Aside from a few shutters and added columns, the house had changed little from the Tudor style favored in the day Sir Walter Raleigh had built it as his summer retreat from the heat and pestilence of London. The distinctive cross beams running from roof to foundation in vee patterns were rotten and badly in need of paint. Many of the mullioned windows needed replacing. But it was home, and the loss of it to an enemy who would sell it or let it rot was a bitter one.

She tilted her head in its jaunty feathered cap and kneed Paris into a gallop, leaving the past behind for an uncertain future. It would be a future, at least, that she would forge.

The Gentle Beast

*   *   *

Her delusion didn't survive the day.

They'd barely unpacked their belongings before there was a knock at the door. Simon jumped up from his seat before the fire. "I'll answer."

In her tiny bedroom, Callista folded her last chemise into the rustic drawers built beneath the straw mattress. "Thanks for coming," she heard Simon say. She eased the drawer shut so she could hear the visitor's reply.

"I hate to see you reduced to this, sir," came a respectful voice.

"I am told it will be good for me," Henry replied. "Sit, man. We've tea brewing."

Callista stiffened. Why had Simon invited Quartermain? Her pride recoiled at the thought of him here. But she tilted her head and glided into the tiny space that served as a living, dining, and kitchen area.

"Good morning, Mr. Quartermain. So kind of you to visit."

He rose so quickly his spindly chair scraped against the clay floor. He bowed over her hand, holding it a second longer than required. "Charming as ever, Miss Raleigh. You grow more lovely every time I see you."

Would that I could say the same of you. Most women would consider Alex Trey Quartermain handsome. He was broad-shouldered, with a shock of blond hair that flopped appealingly over a wide, intelligent forehead. His blue eyes were crystal clear and long-lashed, but Callista had always found his looks insipid. She favored dark men. Worse, something about him had always troubled her. His palms were damp, and his mouth had a perpetual slant that was meant to be charming but that she found sarcastic.

Those long-lashed eyes tended to look down his

29

blade of a nose rather than along it. He was the son of one of the wealthiest cits in England and was, in fact, of noble blood on his mother's side. Perhaps it was his arrogance she found so unappealing—perhaps it was his fawning over all those of higher birth.

Which probably accounted for his strong interest in her. If she were not the direct descendant of Sir Walter Raleigh, she seriously doubted he'd be her most persistent suitor. Despite her equally steady rejections, he was always there with a supporting hand or wandering eye. Maybe one day she would be desperate enough to consider him, though her skin crawled at the very thought.

His money, his looks and his obvious intelligence could not appease her, for her dislike stemmed from one irrefutable fact: he was the dominant march hare of a wild set that had entrapped her sweet younger brother.

On her way to the open hearth where a black kettle bubbled, she answered, "Let me get you some tea." Callista glared at Simon's long legs stretched into her path. He moved them aside, the effort making him grimace, and she knew he had his usual hangover. His handsome young face was drawn, stubbled with dark beard. He was only nineteen, but looked years older.

If he didn't change his habits and his cronies, he might not live to his majority, but he'd turned a deaf ear to her warnings, as he did to his father's. As she prepared the tea, Callista mourned. What had happened to the young lad who trailed her about the estate like an adoring puppy?

The answer was simple: Quartermain and his ilk. And if she became involved in a gaming hell with this man, she'd never be able to avoid him as she had in the past. Simon could only fall deeper under his spell. Yet what choice did they have?

Callista quelled the wish for hemlock to spice Quartermain's tea and handed him the plain delft cup and saucer, careful not to brush his fingers. "And what brings you to us, sir?"

"Why, Simon invited me. To discuss your stepfather's business proposal." Quartermain sipped elegantly, his small finger arched in the air.

Henry cleared his throat. "A bit premature, I fear. We do not know yet whether we can raise our own share of the venture."

"Depending upon what it is, I may be willing to give the go-ahead without collateral. Simon is my best friend." Alex beamed a smile at Simon, who grinned warmly back.

Poppycock! Callista wanted to retort. *You don't make friends; you make tools.* She sipped calmly.

Henry set his cup and saucer down on the raised hearth and drew the lap robe closer about his shoulders. "Our proposal is simple enough. We want to open a new gaming hell."

Slowly Alex lowered his cup. "I see. With the number at present in the city, that would appear to be a risky enterprise. I fear I could not commit much without some form of collateral." His clear blue gaze swung in Callista's direction.

She pretended not to notice and stared into her cup.

Henry replied, "You know we have none."

"Do I?"

Callista's ears began to burn, but still she didn't look up.

Henry followed his stare and sighed. "None, sir. I regret you had a wasted trip on such a chilly day."

Simon levered himself upright. " 'Lista, why don't

you say something? You know right enough what Alex means."

Alex set his cup and saucer down on the floor with a clatter. He rose, advanced on Callista, and stopped before her. "My dear Miss Raleigh, surely you know, after our acquaintance these last two years and more, that my feelings for you remain as constant as the stars."

"The stars, sir, are believed to be constantly moving," Callista answered dryly, abandoning her pretense of deafness. But when Quartermain pried her cup away and set it aside to take her hands, she squirmed out of her chair and rose to face him. "Please do not continue. I am honored at your interest, but my feelings and my troth remain unpledged because I wish it so. I fear I take too much after my great-great-grandmama. I doubt I shall ever wed. Now please excuse me. I wish to check on Paris."

His face had gone carefully blank, but those blue eyes were not quite so clear now. As Callista looked into them, she realized the shadows gathering there were a truer reflection of his soul. Not even to save the estate or to retain Paris could she wed this man. Smiling falsely, she skirted him on her path to the door. "Good day. Have a safe journey back to London."

She busied herself in Paris's stall fluffing up hay and hanging up tack until she heard a horse gallop away. Limp with relief, she dusted off her hands and returned to the cottage.

She expected to be met by Simon's glare, but he flung the door wide when she opened it and hugged her. "I thought we were lost, but damn if you don't make him more eager. He will fund half the venture and ask his friends for more. All we have to do is raise a quarter and agree to run the place. He's going back to London

The Gentle Beast

now to test the waters. We are supposed to go tomorrow. If his friends join in, we can begin to seek appropriate property."

"Jolly good show, Callista." Henry struggled to his feet to buss her cheek.

Callista neither frowned nor smiled, for in truth she didn't know how to react. Every instinct she possessed shrank from being indebted to this man.

Which left her with one alternative. "I am going to London with you."

"Fine. We can use a woman's perspective. We want somewhere respectable, eh, Simon?"

While the two men sat back down before the fire, Callista retreated to her room. She didn't bother correcting them because she knew her stepfather would worry, but she had other plans. She sorted through her trunks, seeking her best gown. Ah, there it was. She shook out the moss gray velvet mantelet and wine-colored taffeta dress. Wishing for a mirror, she held the garments against her.

As armor and weaponry went, they were sufficient. On her visit to Herrick Importers, Ltd., she'd throw down the gauntlet.

Chapter Two

No matter how many times Callista ventured the twenty miles into London from her estate, the city never failed to amaze her. In her own short lifetime, she'd seen vast changes that led to this modern year of 1772: buildings erected, buildings torn down, roads constantly cobbled, others dug up to make squares and residential areas. Top lofty mansions sometimes lorded over cowering tenements. The physical barrier between the two was a grassy sward and an iron fence, but the social barrier was a chasm few tried to bridge and fewer crossed.

From the squalid docks where scavengers and sewer rats battled over morsels, to Hyde Park, where the quality paraded along manicured paths, London was a city of contrasts. Rabble and regent alike attended witty plays and comedies, their laughter equally hearty. Elite coffeehouses rumbled with the learned discourse of Dr. Samuel Johnson and friends; around the corner, pub owners doled out blue ruin, uncaring of the wages exacted or of the attendant sins it visited.

Unlike most of her peers, Callista did not close her eyes or her mind to London's meaner aspects. But she loved London anyway. Surely no other city on earth offered such opportunity cloaked in rags or such penury disguised in silk.

Only in London could a poor boy claw his way from obscurity to adulation as Dr. Johnson had, or an orange-seller become a king's consort, as Nell Gwyn had. For those tireless enough, and brave enough, London offered a better life. As Callista watched the streets lurch past, she reflected that she, for all her birth, was little different from the street vendors plying their wares. She, too, had come here to better herself.

Unfortunately, she, too, elicited her share of interest. Ladies generally did not traverse London in farm carts. Callista held her head high at the curious stares, but Simon pulled his greatcoat up about his chin as they turned onto London's better avenues.

A hawker bellowed to the hurrying pedestrians, "Three a penny Yarmouth bloaters!"

A costermonger, dapper in his silk neckerchief and embroidered boots, had bedecked his donkey in a fine harness that gleamed in the weak winter sunshine. He manned his cart with courtly charm, bowing deeply to his customer, a panniered lady and her velvet-suited son. They sampled the hot chestnuts and returned to their sedan chair. As the lad mounted, a hurrying chimney sweep brushed against him, knocking a nut from his hand. He scowled, but his mother whisked him inside the chair and drew the curtain closed.

The chimney sweep darted a look behind him, and then pounced on the nut. Without bothering to wipe off the grime, he gobbled it down. The man behind him kicked his scrawny buttocks, and the boy went flying.

Callista frowned, preparing to call to Simon to stop the cart, but the lad scrambled to his feet and nimbly avoided another blow, dancing up the street, his master in hot pursuit. He was obviously used to surviving.

And that, Callista thought as she leaned back, was the essence of London's charm and danger. The world's largest city was a veritable cornucopia of opportunity—and despair.

Callista had attended reform meetings with Marian Tupper, an eccentric friend of hers from the select academy they'd attended as young ladies. The Methodists and Quakers there, along with a smattering of her own kind, were well intentioned but impractical. The landed gentry would never institute reforms to limit their own power. The only true change would come politically, led by men brave enough to demand parliamentary reform.

Men like John Wilkes. And look what had happened to him, Callista thought bitterly. Thrice expelled from the Commons despite being legally elected by vast majorities. Prime Minister Lord North ruled well as George III's surrogate, but the discord he'd squashed would rise again. And she, poor or secure, would do what she could to aid it.

"Why the frown, child?" Henry asked.

"Did you see the chimney sweep back there?"

"Lord, don't go into that again," inserted Simon hastily. "M'head's pounding."

"So it should be." Callista crossed her ankles.

"Miss prim and proper," Simon grumbled.

Callista stared unseeingly as a slattern rounded a corner, arm in arm with a man who ducked his head. "No longer, it would seem. How can I condemn vice and commerce when I'm about to involve myself intimately with the very essence of it?"

Simon and Henry exchanged a glance at her grim honesty.

Henry said gently, "You can change your mind, you know. We shall manage somehow. Truly I don't like involving you. The ton will be scandalized. We can hire dealers."

"Dammit, we need her," Simon interjected. "She has the devil's own luck at cards."

"Skill, more like," Henry rebuked him. "Remain in the country if you wish, my child."

Would that it were so simple, Callista thought wearily. What was she to do, preserve hearth and home in the little cottage, or work to regain her stolen lands and good name? She'd quit caring what society thought when it turned its back on Heath. Besides, it was too late for her to raise herself above the fray now. It had become too late when Drake Herrick invaded her home and the scant peace he'd allowed her. He'd thrown the gauntlet at her feet; it was more in her nature to pick it up than to step over it.

"No, Henry," she replied at last. "I have no more choice than you. If you find a likely place, send word to me at Marian's and I will come immediately. I have an errand to run first." *An errand I cannot run alone.*

Unescorted single females were seldom allowed access to a man's business office. But with one of the wealthiest widows in London as chaperon, even the sacred ground of Herrick Importers, Ltd., should be accessible enough. She had a feeling Herrick might refuse to see her, but any businessman would be mad to refuse a visit with the Marchioness of Netham.

When Marian's palatial mansion came into view, Callista gathered up her reticule and tightened her gray mantelet hooks, pulling her fox-trimmed hood over her hair. The footman sauntering down the sweeping front steps went stock-still as he caught sight of who waited to descend. He rushed the rest of the distance, his shooing hand dropping back to his side.

Bug-eyed, he set a box down on the paving and extended his hand to help her alight. "My lady, the mistress said to bring you inside to the parlor as soon as you arrived."

Nodding regally, as had been her wont when, ages past, she'd stepped down from her well-sprung chaise, Callista said over her shoulder, "Good hunting, Henry."

"I shall see you this evening, my dear, if not before." Henry took the reins from Simon's slack hands and clucked to the nag. It lumbered forward.

Callista entered to the comforting scents of beeswax, fresh flowers, and soap. She closed her eyes, assaulted by a rush of homesickness. So her house had smelled once upon a time.

Before the servants went.

Before Drake Herrick came.

"Good afternoon, my lady," said a dignified voice.

Callista opened her eyes to the butler's solemn face. "It is good to see you, Colter. How is your wife?"

"Well, milady. It is kind of you to inquire. Her ladyship awaits you in the salon." Colter led the way to the door off the marble-tiled entryway. The domed ceiling was elaborately stuccoed and painted, exquisite even three stories above. "Lady Callista Raleigh," he intoned as he opened the polished mahogany doors.

A chubby face as cherubic as the cupids cavorting on the mural behind it looked up from an embroidery frame. "Praise the Lord, you're here at last. Delivering me from boredom, as usual."

Callista grinned. "Marian, I thought you'd given up trying to be a proper lady?"

The Gentle Beast

"Oh I have, I have." The little woman stabbed her needle into the tangle of threads and rose, her figure plump but curved in all the right places. "But Elizabeth Downing wagered that I couldn't complete a chair cover in a month's time." She cocked her head critically, eyeing her creation. "Luckily she did not specify in what condition the cover had to be."

Callista chuckled, some of her depression easing. Marian always made her laugh. "You are as susceptible to a wager as ever, I see."

A soft, scented cheek brushed Callista's. "Rather the pot calling the kettle black, is it not?"

Just wait until you hear why I've come. But for now, Callista only hugged her friend back. "No doubt you shall win. The question is, what?"

"A fan, of course. The most exquisite watered silk, which she acquired in Paris."

"Ah, I see." Marian's fan collection was legendary among the ton. Women were constantly agog to see which fan Marian would bring to the latest rout or theater outing. So, Callista thought with an inward grin, were some of the men. The macaronis plied fans with all the skill of the women they flirted with.

Marian drew her to the charming tapestry-backed sofa adjacent to the roaring fire. "But enough of me. Your life is much more interesting. What was so important in your letter that you must be so devilishly secretive?"

"Henry must not know where I am going, but I cannot go alone. What better escort than the Marchioness of Netham?"

"Wheedle all day, my girl, but I will be no part of your scheme unless you tell me all."

Callista chuckled. "Really, Marian, such dignity

comes odd from the same girl who put crickets in the headmistress's soup."

Marian's pretty face, with its dimpled chin and big, Wedgwood blue eyes, did not smile. "And such subterfuge comes odd from the girl who caught them for me."

Callista's smile faded. "I want you to help me gain access to Drake Herrick. I hear he is something of a recluse, but surely even he will not refuse to see the wealthy widow Tupper." Callista's stomach rumbled as she appraised the tray before the sofa. In a measure of her deep friendship with Marian, she helped herself to a scone without waiting for an invitation.

"Herrick!" Marian's eyes grew even larger. "Oh, Callista, do not tell me the Dragon is the one who—"

"Very well, I shall not tell you. Are you coming with me, or not?"

"You know I will, so do not sit upon your high horse."

"Precious good that's done me. I have only the farther to fall, as he has so royally proved." Callista sank her teeth into the warm, soft scone and chewed methodically.

Marian's delicate wheaten brows rose. They were a shade darker than the golden curls piled atop her head. "I have not heard that bitter tone since Heath died."

"You shall likely hear it a lot, unless my plan succeeds."

"Uh-oh." Marian, too, knew Callista well. "My very dear friend, why will you not accept my offer and move in with me? These complex strategies could lead to ruin."

"And I thank you again, my very dear friend, but I cannot rest until I have my estate back. After all these years, I will not lose it now. Especially to such a one." Callista set the half-eaten scone on her plate. "Strategy is indispensable to a successful campaign. Herrick has fired the opening salvo, but the battle is just beginning."

"You talk like you're at war."

"And so I am. My very way of life is at stake, after all." Callista explained in full detail her encounter with Herrick two nights before.

Accepting the inevitable, Marian picked up a china plate and piled it with a scone, fruit compote, and two kidneys. "My word, he does sound sinister. Why on earth does he hate Henry so?" She cut into the fork-tender kidney and took a delicate bite.

"I don't know. But I mean to find out."

"Let me fortify myself while you tell me your battle plan." While she ate, Callista talked.

The ormolu clock on the mantel marked off an hour by the time Callista was finished. "Well, shall you help me?"

Marian was frowning. "I suppose if I refuse, you will find another way." Marian wiped her hands and mouth with a lace-trimmed napkin.

Callista shrugged.

"Minx."

Callista bowed from the waist.

"Very well. You may have your match here. If Henry succeeds in this insane endeavor, you will daily challenge unmarried men to cards. I will do what I can to help, of course, but your good name will be ruined among many. But then, you know that and obviously do not care."

Callista shook her head. "I stopped caring what society thought the day Heath died defending me from the tattlemongers."

Sighing, Marian continued, "However, the second part of your plan concerns me. Drake Herrick is vastly rich, vastly powerful, and vastly strange. He has refused every hostess in London. No one even knows where he lives. He obviously values his privacy. I have no doubt he will be a trifle put out with you if you invade his home, assuming you can even find it."

That was a masterly understatement, Callista thought. She recalled the strength he radiated from his strong ankles to his perfect mouth. She quelled a shiver. "What have you heard about him?"

"Rumors abound, but little of substance is known. Only a handful of people have seen the man. He does seem to enjoy cards, but he only plays with business associates, and he never takes off his mask."

Callista frowned. She'd assumed he'd used the mask that night at her house for effect. This time the shiver crawled up her spine like a warning. And most effective that dragon mask had been. Was he hideous, or did he fear recognition?

As she digested the information, her resolve hardened. Any man who went about in a mask and refused to let anyone know where he lived had something to hide. Something that could be used against him. If she felt a qualm at contemplating blackmail, that, too, she squelched. He had ruthlessly stolen all she valued. Why should she balk at using the same tactics? She gathered her scattered attention as Marian went on.

"Those who have spoken with him say he has much the air and speech of an aristocrat, yet no one knows of any noble Herricks."

"I would certainly agree that he comes from a noble background. But as you well know, nobility and goodness seldom go hand in hand." Callista leaped up. "Well, time's short. Shall I help you get ready?"

Marian rose more slowly. "What if you lose Paris? I know how much he means to you."

42

The Gentle Beast

"I shall not. But I have to risk him. I know of no other way to raise the funds, short of taking to the road."

"If you would let me—"

Callista hugged her friend, who was half a head shorter. "Generous to a fault as you are, I cannot take advantage of you. The venture will be risky, to say the least. And should it become known you were part owner of a gaming hell, think of the scandal."

"I am." Marian looked grimly up at Callista.

Swinging about, Callista led the way into the entry. "Ah, but I am already disapproved. Raising my own racehorse, owning my own estate—"

"Neither of which compares to running a gaming hell. How will you ever make a suitable match then?"

Callista gave her a look that made Marian crinkle her nose. "Oh, very well, I shall hush. But you may love again, someday."

"No."

The word echoed with finality in the foyer, but Marian's pretty face was worried as she climbed the stairs, calling for her dresser.

Callista didn't notice her friend's concern as she trailed back into the parlor. She saw only Heath's face, as vivid in her mind's eye as if two years had not passed since he died in the duel over her good name. Heath of the laughing eyes and the kind heart. Callista put her knuckles to her mouth to stifle a moan.

No, she had no fear she'd love again. What she made of her life involved no one save herself, Henry, and Simon. If she lost her reputation in becoming mistress of her destiny again, so be it. Not grief, not propriety, not even fear itself would stop her from reclaiming what was hers. . . .

*   *   *

Herrick Importers, Ltd., was located in splendid quarters on the spanking clean New Bond Street, which extended north from the original street. The building occupied half a block, with a luxurious shop on the front, a warehouse in the back, and, Callista assumed as she peeked out of Marian's carriage, the offices on the second floor. The day was growing gloomy, so she could see that every window was lit from within.

The carriage door opened. Marian handed the footman one of her elegant, engraved calling cards. "Tell Mr. Drake Herrick I request an audience."

He bowed, straightened his green and gold livery, and disappeared inside the shop. A bell tinkled pleasantly, and the two women watching at the window noticed that the footman was immediately met by a sales clerk. The young man peered out the bow window, and then hurried off.

"It certainly looks prosperous," Marian observed. "That window glass must have been shockingly dear. And have you ever noticed a nicer display? I have often wondered why more merchants do not try to entice shoppers inside by glassing in their fronts and artfully arranging their wares."

The whole establishment, even from this distance, bespoke breeding and wealth. Callista clenched her hands inside her silver fox muff, reminding herself of the generations of blue blood flowing through her veins.

The footman, escorted by the sales clerk, returned quickly. The young man bowed deeply. "Please, your ladyship, if you'll come with me, I'll escort you to the master's office."

"Excellent, good fellow." Marian tripped down the carriage steps. "My friend comes with me, of course."

The Gentle Beast

The sales clerk looked a bit doubtful, but he didn't refute her.

The inside of the shop was even more impressive. Red velvet curtains trimmed in gold decorated every window; thick green carpeting embellished with moss-colored roses cushioned their feet. Exquisite chandeliers above their heads, row upon row, would have cast enough light to illuminate Westminster at dusk.

Callista noticed that each chandelier was affixed with a discreet label. She squinted against the light. When she read the amount on the smallest chandelier, she gasped. Obviously everything in the shop was of the best quality.

The cases they passed held a vast array of accessories, from snuffboxes, to watches, to fobs and opera glasses. Precious jewels glittered from more cases against the wall. In the back of the shop, imported furniture was artfully arranged. A marquetry secretary from Italy shared an oriental rug with a black-lacquered desk and ivory-inlaid chair.

Marian paused to pick up a gold saltcellar. "This looks like a Cellini," she said, turning the figure of Neptune astride a sea serpent over in her hands.

"It is, milady."

Carefully, Marian set the figure back down, rolling her eyes at the price dangling from the serpent's tail. "Quaint custom, marking everything," she whispered to Callista. "Herrick certainly is not in the usual habit of haggling, is he? Take it or leave it, as it were."

The entire shop reflected that philosophy, yet business certainly didn't seem to suffer. Elegantly dressed men and women wandered the vast premises, touching and lifting, debating. The contents of one of those jewel cases, Callista realized bitterly, would probably buy back her entire estate. Any man who could afford to stock such ware must have wealth beyond her comprehension.

Dresden figurines cavorted atop an elaborately carved teak table that was inlaid with mother-of-pearl. An immense bedstead of some strange design sat next to it. As she passed the bed on the way to the stairs, Callista was astonished to realize that the bedposts were made of ivory tusks. By the time they reached the landing at the next level, Callista's head was spinning.

Outside a heavy oak door marked *Drake Herrick, Esq.*, Callista paused. She met Marian's eyes, smiling faintly as Marian lifted her chin and tapped the underside of Callista's. Obediently, Callista set her head at a proud angle as the door was opened to the clerk's knock.

The interior of the office reeked of wealth, masculinity, and arrogance, but Callista noticed little besides a vague impression of leather, tobacco, and expensive furniture. She held her breath as a figure rose from behind the desk, then expelled it in disappointment. This man was far too old and dignified to be Drake Herrick. He ushered both ladies into the brass-studded chairs before the vast desk.

"How may I help you, ladies? Clyde Haynes, Mr. Herrick's business manager, at your service." His full head of gray hair was unpowdered, though neatly tied at his nape. His worn face was still handsome, as full of character and breeding as the room around him. He wore black from head to toe, an affectation doubtless learned from his master, Callista thought tartly.

The two women exchanged a glance.

Marian said slowly, "I had hoped to see Mr. Herrick himself."

"He seldom does business directly anymore. I assure

The Gentle Beast

you I have his full authority to act as his surrogate. Do you wish to refurbish a house? Purchase some jewelry? We are delighted at your interest in our establishment."

At a pleading glance from Callista, Marian said loftily, "Very well, I'd like to see some of your pearls, please. The quality of the ones I've seen heretofore has simply been inadequate. I wish to have the best service, of course, instead of making do with the rabble." Marian rose, winking at Callista as the manager rounded the desk.

Smothering her mirth at Marian's false snobbery, Callista began to stand as well. Instead, she put the back of her hand to her forehead, groaned, and fell into the chair. "My head again, Marian."

Marian put a cool hand against Callista's forehead. "You are a touch warm. Rest. I shall not be long." Marian swept to the doorway in a regal rustle of silk rubbing against hoops. She glanced over her shoulder, lifting an eyebrow, when Mr. Haynes hovered over Callista, reaching for a corner of the desk as he did so.

A bell jangled somewhere in the distance, but Callista assumed it was the one attached to the shop door.

Bowing, Haynes finally opened the door for Marian and ushered her out.

The second the door closed, Callista erupted into action.

She tried the desk first, but the side drawers held only boring ledgers, accounts, and bills of sale. The top drawer yielded quills, spare nibs, ink pots, vellum, seals, and wax. Innocuous enough.

Frustrated, Callista slammed the drawer closed. She froze as she thought she heard a footstep, but, when the sound didn't come again, she dismissed it as a thump from downstairs. She scanned the room. Bookcases fronted the left wall beside the desk, but on closer examination, she saw that they held only assorted novels, plays, and tomes on such weighty matters as textiles, antiquities, and jewelry.

Her eye lit on the secretary against the wall behind the door. She hurried over and flipped down the top. To her delight, she found several locked drawers. Rushing back to the desk, she filched the letter opener from the top desk drawer and hurried back to the secretary. They'd be back soon, and Lord knew when she'd have such an opportunity again.

She was prying at the delicate lock, trying not to mar the fruitwood, when a click and a whoosh sounded at her back. Callista froze.

"Find anything interesting?" asked a voice Callista remembered well.

The letter opener dropped from her numb fingers. Slowly Callista turned, bracing her hands on the open lid behind her. Again he seemed to stride from the demon regions, for a black hole gaped in the wall behind him where the bookcase had swung outward.

This time he wore no cloak. His black silk shirt and black nankeen breeches molded his awesome physique in loving detail. His dragon mask was whimsical rather than menacing this time. Of red velvet, it was sewn with jet at eyebrows and ears. In a measure of his masculinity, he still looked dangerously male wearing the frippery. His hair, drawn back at his neck with a simple leather cord, was as black as a dragon's wing, thick and shining, with all the vitality of its owner.

Callista bit her lip, searching for some excuse, but there simply was none. "Not yet. Should you go out the way you came in, however, I may yet prevail."

He went still, and then kicked the bookcase closed with his boot. "You, my dear, are as bold a piece as I've

48

come across." He sauntered forward. Muscles rippled under his form-fitting clothes, and again Callista had the impression that this man was more beast than human.

She stood her ground, however, even when he was within touching range, even when he reached out. . . . She gasped. A small brass key dangled from a dragon-headed key chain. To her shock he stepped around her and opened all the tiny drawers.

He moved back, swept his arm before him, and bowed. "Anything to please a lady."

Callista stared up at him, wishing she could rip his mask and subterfuge away. He obviously expected to shame her, but he had a thing or two to learn about her. Whirling, she opened the nearest drawer. Ivory dice and a throwing box, cards. The next drawer yielded a pile of guineas. The last drawer, the wide middle one, held nothing but a long book. She snatched it out, waiting for him to take it away, but he merely crossed his arms and watched her.

She flipped through the well thumbed, yellowing pages. The book was obviously very old. Her breath hissed through her teeth. A flush started at her hairline and spread to her toes. Damn him, he'd wanted her to find this. Instead of dropping the book as she longed to do, she forced herself to casually scan the title. *The Kama Sutra.* The title meant nothing to her, but the drawings gave her an odd feeling in her lower extremities. Especially in *his* presence. "Rather pedestrian artwork, actually." She kept her head lowered so he wouldn't see her flush.

The depictions of the sexual act were varied and explicit, but the joining of male to female had a certain raw power, a passion that leaped from the pages.

He appraised her, head cocked on one side. "The pictures obviously hold no surprises for you. That should make it easier."

Discomfitted, Callista set the book back down. "Make what easier?"

"Our contest. I am delighted you have accepted my challenge. I suspected you would." He moved a step nearer.

She backed up until the secretary lid ground into her spine. Suspicion darkened her lovely green eyes. "What the deuce are you talking about?"

"Such language." Propping both hands on the lid behind her, effectively caging her, he dipped his head until his breath, scented of mint and coffee, brushed her hot cheeks. "I knew you would come, though I did not expect you so quickly. Clyde had strict instructions to escort you to the office and leave you here alone—"

"In your lair!"

"—because I wanted to see which image of you was true before we proceeded with our delightful little game." He tipped her chin up with a warm, leather-gloved finger. "The proper lady, heiress of Sir Walter Raleigh, or the vixen who breeds her own racehorse, Henry's daughter in all but name."

Callista didn't need to ask which impression he'd garnered. Under the circumstances, she could hardly protest her innocence. Besides, moral rectitude would not serve her purposes. "Censure from a man afraid to show his face is rather a paradox, you must admit."

"Oh, freely. But you misunderstand. I do not criticize. I am actually quite delighted to find you as amoral as your stepfather. I can proceed with a clear conscience." His disturbingly beautiful mouth lowered slowly toward hers.

Callista lifted her half boot and brought it smartly down on his toe. When he winced, she nimbly stepped

The Gentle Beast

out of the loosened circle of his arms. "You will proceed straight to hell if you allow your 'conscience' to
guide you. I shall certainly not seek perdition with
you."

A big hand caught her waist as she spun toward the
door. Effortlessly, he spun her back, pulling her so
close that her gray clothing blended with his black.
"But you shall. Any woman with a dog named Cerberus
should know better than to cross the river Styx. But
now that you have, like Persephone, you shall find,
eventually, that the devil makes stimulating company.
For example . . ."

Destiny waited for her on his lips. She strained to
pull away, but that only made it easier for him to arch
her over his arm. She braced herself, expecting to be
brutalized, but his lips were warm, mobile, appreciative. He brushed his own compelling contours against
her feminine ones from lips to ankles, silk sliding
against velvet. His touch conveyed artistry only experience taught, and Callista was far more innocent than
he knew. . . .

Callista's toes curled at the erotic touch of velvet
against her face, and silk-wrapped steel under her fingers where she clutched his shoulders. He swallowed
her startled little catch of breath and trailed his mouth
down her arched throat, only to return insatiably to
her tingling lips. The kiss deepened. He caught her
wrists and lifted her arms about his neck, pulling her
off her feet, his mouth ravaging the last of her reserve.

Helplessly she dangled there. The room faded as feelings grew. It had been so long since she felt warm,
wanted, that she had no room for struggle, or even de-
nial. Enemy though he was, ruthless though he was,
dear heaven, this man could kiss! She began to kiss
him back, years of loneliness easing in the cherished

51

Colleen Shannon

clutch of strong, needful arms.

A husky little laugh quivered through him when she slanted her mouth more firmly over his. He reached out a long arm and she heard a lock click. He lifted those mesmerizing lips long enough to sweep her up into his arms and walk with her toward the hidden stairway. "Softly, vixen, we need not hurry."

"Heath . . ." she sighed, her mouth buried against a throbbing neck that seemed so familiar, so enticing. Heath, too, had been fond of peppermints.

Those long strides stopped. The carpet met her feet in a jarring thud that made her eyes fly open. He pulled her arms from about his neck and stood back.

"Do not call me by your lover's name," he said softly, dangerously. "The only name upon your mouth when I take you will be my own."

The words banished the last sweet wisps of rapture. This man was truly a demon. Only some sorcerer could make her mistake him, even for an instant, for her sweet, honorable Heath. "Beast! You will never—"

He caught the front of her mantelet and pulled her close to stick that whimsical, magical face into her own. "Beast I may be, but thank your stepfather for my creation. I have his fortune, I have his lands, and soon I shall have his daughter."

When she batted at his hand, he released her. She wrapped her wounded dignity about her like her cape and stood tall, generations of pride strengthening her spine. "Since you obviously like challenges, sir, I invite you to a rubber of piquet. I stake my racehorse, Paris, against your deed to my estate and five thousand pounds."

He leaned his slim hips against the desk. "Rather an unequal bet, even if Paris is the brother of Eclipse. No, I fear I must demand further collateral."

52

The Gentle Beast

That glittering gaze was so alive with male desire that she felt physically touched where it lit, at mouth, breasts, and ankles. She pretended obtuseness. "I have nothing else of value, except . . ." She looked down at the ring on her finger. It was a large, square-cut emerald, perfect and unadorned. It was rumored to have been a gift from Queen Bess herself to her favorite courtier—before he fell out of favor. She'd vowed to starve before she sold it. Recklessly, she took it off and offered it to him on her palm.

"I have this. It has been in my family since the days of Sir Walter himself. Good Queen Bess supposedly gave it to him when she gifted him with the Irish estate. It is all I have left of the family heirlooms."

He picked it up and took it to the lantern, turning it this way and that. "Excellent quality. But it is not what I want." Returning, he held the ring out. "You know what I want." Again that gaze ran over her, lingering, possessing.

Callista snatched the ring and put it back on. "There are some things even the fierce Dragon cannot have. How pathetic that a man of your stature should be reduced to such bargaining. If I did not find you so deplorable, I could almost pity you."

The hiss of his breath was her only warning before she felt the full force of the Dragon's fury. One minute he was relaxed against the desk; the next he was hovering over her, words of righteous wrath spewing from his mouth like flames. "Pity me, revile me, even hate me, but you will only delay what became inevitable the other night. I have no need of bargaining, or even coercion, as you yourself have proved these moments past in my arms. You will come to me soon enough. Not because you have to—because you want to."

Horrified at what she'd aroused, Callista eased back

toward the door, but for every step she retreated, he advanced.

His voice softened, not to a threat, but to a vow. "We are bound, you and I, in ways you cannot dream of. I will fill you, waking and sleeping, first in your thoughts. Next I will fill your body on my way to your heart. And finally, I will fill your soul and chain you to me, utterly and forever. Whether we know heaven or hell is up to you."

The door, thank God, the door. Callista fumbled with the latch, but couldn't grasp it with her sweaty fingers. He reached around her. She flinched, but heard the latch lift free. Gently he pulled her away so he could open the door.

"Go," he murmured. "I accept your bet. Where shall we meet?"

The corridor was reassuringly wide, tilting her back to equilibrium in its rows of wall scones and geometric-patterned runner. Callista backed away another two steps. A good ten feet stretched between them, and the stairs were but a step away, before she felt safe. "Ah, the Marchioness of Netham has agreed to let us use her home."

"When?"

"Tomorrow. Seven?"

"Agreed." He turned his head as two treads ascended the stairs. "Ah, Clyde. And this lovely lady must be the Marchioness of Netham. How delighted I am to have you on my premises." He sidestepped Callista and met Marian at the head of the stairs. He bowed deeply over her hand. "Drake Herrick, at your service."

Marian's dilated eyes darted back and forth between the two figures: Callista so still and white, Herrick urbane and calm. She cleared her throat and touched the pearls at her neck. "I fear I cannot claim delight. The visit was a costly one for me."

Herrick chuckled. "They are of the first quality, matched from the South Seas, but they hardly do justice to their wearer."

Marian smiled, her eyes trying to pierce the mask. Unsuccessful, she advanced and took Callista's hand. "Ready, my dear?"

Callista managed a nod and turned for the stairs.

"I look forward to the morrow, Lady Raleigh." Herrick opened his office door and disappeared.

Callista wished heartily that he'd leave on the ill wind that had brought him. She marched down the stairs, out to the carriage, Marian's shorter legs hurrying to catch up. When they were safely inside, Marian barraged her with questions.

"But where did he come from? What did he say to you? I take it he accepted your bet? He seems quite charming instead of sinister."

Callista shivered and sank her hands deep into her muff. "You would not say that if you'd come upon us five minutes prior."

"Was he forward?" Marian clapped her hands. "How delightful. If he is interested in you, perhaps he will desist from this senseless persecution."

Callista feared the opposite. She stared unseeingly out the window at the passing shops. His warning was emblazoned on her brain. He seemed almost obsessed with bedding her. She didn't fool herself that his intention went further than that, and she also knew her looks were secondary to his real desire: vengeance. It was Callista, daughter of Henry, that he wanted to use and humble, rather than Callista Raleigh.

She started when Marian touched her arm. Her cherubic face was as serious as it ever got. "My dear, what did he say to cause you such distress?"

"He was expecting me. He opened his secretary himself for me to search. I found . . . nothing of import." She ducked her head and ran the muff over her hot cheek, forbidden images writhing in her mind. Not even to Marian could she relate the menace he conveyed, or her own confusion at responding to him, or the fear lapping at her fingertips.

Dear God, what had she done?

How could she challenge this . . . beast and hope to win?

By the time she'd supped with Marian on stuffed pheasant, duchesse potatoes, and imported oranges, her nerves had settled to grim determination. Drake Herrick had been right about one thing: this day they'd both crossed the river Styx. But if he were going to make her life hellish, then by God he would suffer in return.

The butler knocked and entered at Marian's command. "Your ladyship, the Earl of Swanlea and his son wish an audience."

Marian wiped her mouth. "Send them in, Colter. Have the steward set two more places."

Henry's face was drawn with weariness when he sat down, but he nodded at her inquiring glance. "Found the perfect place." He took a sip of his turtle soup.

Callista talked desultorily with Marian while the two men ate. When their plates had been removed and the comfit dish set on the table, Marian nodded at Henry. "Do you wish us to retire so you can enjoy your port?"

"Not tonight, Marian. I do, however, thank you for the lovely supper." Henry rose. "I need to show Callista the property we found, so I must steal her away. If we do not act soon, we may not get the opportunity to bid.

The Gentle Beast

The place is a bargain, only recently on the market because its owner is in debt."

Marian raised an eyebrow. "Do you speak of the Kimball town house?"

Callista froze in the act of rising, looking at Henry.

He didn't meet her eyes as he went to the door. "Indeed. How did you know?"

Marian was privy to the details of the long-ago scandal, Callista knew.

"Lucky guess," she answered dryly. She walked them to the front entrance, watching as Callista accepted her mantelet and muff from the butler. Henry helped her on with the cape.

"Have my carriage brought 'round, Colter," Marian ordered. She waved away Henry's halfhearted protests. "It looks like snow. None of you need to rattle about in an open conveyance. Will you be spending the night, Henry? You are always welcome."

"I had planned for us to return to the country, Marian."

Marian frowned. "The highwaymen on the north road have been confoundedly bold of late."

"We brought weapons. We have much to plan if we are to open by the end of the month. We could not so impose upon you."

"That fast?" Callista straightened her bonnet. "Surely we should wait until closer to the Season. We cannot have much clientele until the weather warms."

"Precisely why we should open now. Some of the other hells are closed. Gives us an opportunity. Quartermain insisted we open as soon as possible."

And what Quartermain wants, Quartermain gets. Why was she ever surrounded by opportunistic males? Callista drew her mantelet closed, tying it so tight she coughed. She loosened it. "You and Simon may return

57

if you wish, but I'm staying with Marian for a few nights." She hugged her friend. "I shan't be late, Marian."

"Colter will await you. Good evening, everyone." The ornately carved doors closed behind them.

"But Callista, we need your help," Simon protested, following Callista down the steps to the carriage. "There are draperies to order, rooms to decorate—"

"All of which I can do best from London." Callista studied the passing street lanterns.

Henry watched her narrowly. "What has happened today? You were opposed to staying with Marian just this morning."

Henry had already made his disapproval of the wager known, so Callista shrugged. "A whim of mine. Even practical-minded women are allowed them occasionally."

"Why do I have the feeling that your plan is eminently impractical?"

"Like father, like daughter. Am I to believe sheer coincidence led you to the Kimball town house?"

Chapter Three

Henry blustered, "If we want to draw a select clientele, this is the best place. Isn't that so, Simon?"

"Yes. Why must you always be so deuced straitlaced, 'Lista?"

Because one of us has to be. An image of herself dangling in Drake Herrick's embrace flashed across her mind. She rubbed the muff against her cheek again, glad that the carriage was dim. She protested no further, for she was no hypocrite. Besides, the die was cast. She smiled grimly. Literally, in this case.

Callista accepted Henry's hand down from the carriage and paused with him outside the wrought-iron fence to look up at the town house. The grounds were stark; the front door needed painting; several of the slate roof tiles were missing. Nevertheless, harmony resounded in every regal line. Chimneys balanced each end of the rectangular house. An ornate cornice topped the front door, but aside from some fancy brickwork, the house was largely unadorned.

"Inigo Jones himself is rumored to have designed the house, according to the barrister who showed us the property," Henry explained, opening the front door with a large key. At her raised eyebrow, he added, "I am to return the key tomorrow when I make him our offer."

"Has Quartermain seen the place?"

"I intend to show it to him in the morning."

"Why is it available?" In the entry, Callista turned in a slow circle. The arched balustrade curved to the upper level from the parquet-floored entry. Callista didn't see the plaster walls, cracked and dingy, or smell the mustiness of neglect; she saw the spacious lower chambers aglitter with hundreds of candles, dice rattling and cards shuffling. Truly, this place could make for a gaming palace more than a hell.

"Does it come with the furniture?" she asked as she ascended the stairs.

"Yes. Obviously another advantage. I haven't inspected all the furniture yet, but some of it is more than adequate."

Callista noted that the wall curving with the stairway held paler rectangles at intervals and deduced that paintings were missing. "And why is the Kimball heir selling it?"

"To settle his debts. When Bryant Kimball and his son died the estates went to a remote cousin who knew little of land management. He's run through all the ready and now is selling off the assets in an attempt to keep the landed estate."

How sad. Simon had gone into the study off the entryway and now played the pianoforte there. It was badly out of tune, and the music made a macabre accompaniment, echoing through the house like a dirge

The Gentle Beast

devoted to human stupidity. But then, Callista reflected, she could hardly blame the Kimball heir too
much for mismanagement, could she?

She knew little of Bryant Kimball, but her mother
had always seemed in awe of him and regretted her
part in the scandal that ended with his death. He must
have been a proud man. No doubt it would pain him
to see the London house that had been in his family
for over a hundred years sold to the very man he most
detested.

Callista examined both the upstairs quarters and the
top floor, which was partly reserved for servants, partly
used for storage. She and Henry appraised every nook
and cranny, but they found no sign of rot or moisture.

"The roof must be sound," Callista said in relief,
turning. She heard a ripping sound. She knelt and
worked at her skirt, but it was caught on an angular
piece of wood.

"Hold the lantern here so I can see what I'm doing,
please, Henry." Henry complied, and finally she
worked the taffeta free of what she realized now was
a cracked gilt frame. Whatever picture it held was
propped, face forward, against a rickety old table. Using the table to brace herself, she stood. The frame fell
with a thud, sending up a cloud of dust.

She coughed, waving her hand before her face, but
Henry made a choking sound. Concerned, she took a
step toward him before she realized he wasn't choking
on dust. She tilted her head, following his example, to
see the portrait.

A tall man, with a face too strong for handsomeness
and a body too muscular for a lord, stood on the front
stoop of the house. One hand rested on the head of a
hunting dog; the other held the hand of a dark-haired
miniature of himself of about eight. The artist would

61

never be in Gainsborough's league, which probably accounted for why the picture had not been sold, but still the painter had captured both the latent power of the adult and the adoring face the young boy turned up to his father. The way the man stood, legs spread with authority, handclasp firm, was eloquent of both protection and confidence.

Callista glanced at the bottom of the portrait, unsurprised to find the plate reading, *What I have, I hold.* No doubt the Kimball motto.

She glanced from the picture to her stepfather's pale face. "It is Bryant Kimball, is it not?"

He was still staring at the portrait and didn't answer. His expression troubled Callista, for she read a volatile mixture of regret, dislike, and yearning.

"Henry, what is wrong?"

He started and lowered the lantern, turning for the door that led back to the living quarters. "Nothing. Come, my dear."

Somehow, Callista couldn't leave the portrait wallowing in the dust. She set it carefully back against the table, face outward this time. She glanced one last time at the portrait before the light dimmed. Even as shadows took that strong face, the clarity of the bond between father and son grew in her mind.

She hurried after Henry. "Henry, that was Kimball, wasn't it?"

"Yes."

For some reason, now that she'd finally seen a picture of the man her mother had once been engaged to, she felt like an invader. If this man had lived, he would not welcome her, and he most certainly would not want Henry to set foot in his home.

As she descended the stairs, she imagined the domicile alive with childish laughter as the boy chased a dog, the father's indulgent smile as he set aside his book to hug his son. A brief happiness that would end in blood staining the Indian Ocean . . .

"Callista! Answer me." Henry squeezed her hand.

Callista blinked and found herself in the entryway again. "What did you say?"

"I asked if you approve."

Chilled, Callista pulled her loose mantelet closer about her shoulders. "I . . . am not sure. It seems wrong somehow to buy this place now that I have seen the man it once belonged to."

"Nonsense. We shall find nothing better. The young wastrel is in such dire need that we should be able to negotiate a good price."

"But is it one we can meet? How do you intend to raise our portion?"

Henry's hand went to the stickpin at his throat. Even in the dim glow of the few candles the barrister had allowed them, the diamond glittered.

"Henry, no!"

His hand dropped. "I have lost your own fortune. The least I can do is sell all I have of value in an effort to win it back."

Callista debated telling him about her game, but decided not to. He'd be too busy with Quartermain tomorrow to sell the stone. And if she won, she could delight in telling him that she'd raised the funds herself. Surely five thousand pounds would cover their part of the deposit.

She covered her yawn. "Shall we worry about that when we must? I am quite fatigued. It is frightfully late for you to insist on traveling back to Summerlea. I know sheer pride is making you stubborn. Stay the night at Marian's."

Simon exited the study. "She's right, as usual, Fa-

Colleen Shannon

ther. We've much to do tomorrow." Simon helped his sister extinguish all the candles and lanterns, and then held the door for her.

As Henry locked it behind them, he said wearily, "Very well, if Marian is not too inconvenienced."

Callista smiled. "Knowing Marian, she'll have your beds waiting for you."

Indeed, Callista knew Marian exceedingly well.

The next morning, when Henry and Simon had left, she discovered anew that Marian, in turn, knew her friend equally well.

"Callista," she said, swallowing a bit of scone, "your birthday is at hand, and I saw the most perfect dress for you at Madame Josette's." Innocent blue eyes blinked winsomely at Callista over a delicate porcelain teacup.

This time, Callista vowed, Marian's sweet generosity would not soften her. Her friend wanted her to look her best for tonight. She knew Callista's gowns were a year out of fashion, but Marian was far too astute to try the direct approach.

"Most kind of you, Marian, but you have already done too much for me." Callista set her own cup down properly in her saucer, pretending not to hear Marian's forlorn sigh.

"I was so looking forward to shopping with you. You have seldom been into town of late."

"I shall accompany you gladly, but you will not purchase me anything."

Marian nibbled at a slice of orange. Delicately she licked her lips, adding in an offhand manner, "The dress is red. Trimmed in jet. Wickedly proper."

Callista shoved her cup—and temptation—away. "Unfair! You know how much I love red."

The Gentle Beast

"Assuredly. And I also know how well you wear it." Marian tilted her head as she examined her friend. "I declare it is odd. With that red hair the color should clash dreadfully, but somehow it brings out your complexion. Must hint of your true nature."

"An example of which you shall shortly see if you don't desist." Callista gave her friend a mock grimace.

Marian covered her delightful, gurgling laugh with her napkin. "I only want you to do me and my home proud this eve. And since you attained your majority, it is not improper for you to wear red."

"And for my new calling, it should be most appropriate," Callista said before she thought.

Marian clapped her hands and rose. "Famous! I knew you could not resist."

"But Marian . . ." Callista was still protesting when they arrived at the shop.

At exactly seven, Callista heard voices downstairs. She cupped her stomach, but the butterflies only fluttered more wildly. "I must have been mad. What if I lose?"

"What if you win?" Marian countered. "Drake Herrick, I remind you, is not accustomed to losing."

"He can hardly do any more to me than he already has."

Marian lifted an eyebrow at this bravado, looking more than ever like an inquisitive sprite. "There speaks an innocent who knows little of strong men." Then, smiling, she added slyly, "But since I suspect Drake Herrick knows little of strong women, perhaps he has met his match."

"Marian," Callista said, sweeping her friend a deep curtsy, "you are ever the punster, but in this instance

I adore your turn of phrase. Shall we hope it forecasts good luck?"

When a knock came at the door, Marian called, "Tell Mr. Herrick we shall be right down."

"Very good, milady." The servant's steps retreated.

At the door, Marian caught her friend's arm, her lovely face serious now. "Callista, even if you fail, I want you to know nothing would delight me more than for you and Henry and Simon to move in with me."

Callista's throat tightened. Such friends came along only once in a lifetime. If the situation were reversed, she'd do the same for Marian. And precisely because Callista loved Marian so much, she could not take advantage of her. No, if their last desperate gamble failed, they'd best learn to like being country bumpkins. She shook her head wordlessly, but softened the refusal with a hug.

Marian sighed and held Callista away by the arms. "Oh very well, I will badger you no more. At least you let me buy you the dress. I knew it would be perfect for you." Marian opened the door and twirled her index finger.

Obediently Callista moved out in the hall to give her hoops room, and turned slowly. She did feel wonderful in the dress and knew she'd seldom looked so good. Only silk this fine shimmered with every minute movement, changing from pale red to burgundy depending on the angle of the light. Powdering was an affectation Callista used only on the grandest occasions, so her hair, piled high and ornamented with a red velvet rose, added to the impression that she was a living flame.

Her black corset was trimmed in black lace scattered with jet, and the trim peeped at the heart-shaped neckline. The cut would have been prim save that the deep flounce moved with her every breath, offering a tantalizing glimpse of cleavage as she breathed out, then, as she breathed in, bolstering her modesty again. Her black petticoats were similarly bedecked and showed in the front, where the red layers were swept to the sides and tied with black lace bows.

Marian chuckled. "If you do not distract him in that dress, he is a man of iron. But just in case . . ."

Marian walked with Callista toward the stairs, ducked into her own room, then hurried back out. She handed Callista a fan. "It is one of my favorites."

Callista turned it over in her hands. The delicate supports were black mother-of-pearl, the material black silk. Embroidered on the silk was the pattern of a single red rose, half open, lush with life and beauty.

"It is not expensive. Please keep it. It goes divinely with the dress."

"Thank you, Marian. I could not have a better friend."

Downstairs, Marian led the way into the salon where she'd had the servants set up a small gaming table she kept for parties. She gestured for Callista to wait, whispering to Colter, "Announce her when I say 'ready.' " She disappeared inside.

Callista heard her say, "Good evening, Mr. Herrick. May I offer you refreshment?"

"Thank you, no. I never drink and play."

"Very well. If you are ready, then . . ."

Colter swept the double doors wide open. "Lady Callista Antonia Raleigh."

The fan resting at her side like a sheathed sword, Callista glided into the room. Marian had arranged the candelabra to illuminate the front of the room, where the table was set before the fireplace, so Callista had to blink at the abrupt blaze of light.

When her eyes adjusted, she saw that Drake Herrick

had gone curiously still. She sensed the sweep of his gaze, but her own breath caught as she, too, could not hide her interest. In boots and breeches he was impressive, but in formal dress, he was . . . stunning. Every item he wore, from his single gold watch and fob to the expensive white silk stockings and sapphire buckles on his shoes, was of the first stare of fashion.

However, Callista noticed less his good taste and more the way he wore it: like one born to sapphires and silk. Even more distracting was the manly shape the form-fitting garments revealed. His royal blue coat accentuated his massive shoulders. His legs seemed to go on forever, from shapely ankles, to strong calves, to the black silk knee breeches hugging his muscular thighs. A sapphire-and-diamond stickpin glittered at his snowy neckcloth. Lace peeped out from his sleeves. His gloves were formal white this time, and even his missing fingers could not detract from the sheer power of his presence. His pale blue mask offered a dragon more humorous than horrible.

His lips, the only feature the mask revealed, lifted in a sardonic smile.

He knew she was admiring him. She snapped her fan open and executed a deep curtsy, all the while telling herself it would not do for her to be attracted to this man. Drake Herrick's empire rested upon his ability to exploit the weaknesses of others. Tonight, of all nights, she didn't dare forget that.

"Good evening," she said calmly.

He bowed. "May I be so bold as to say you are delightfully in looks tonight?"

Callista rose from her curtsy, fanning herself so that only her eyes were revealed. "May I be so bold as to say the same of you? I much prefer you in blue rather than black."

The Gentle Beast

"And red is more your true color than gray."

Satisfied that her guests had all they needed, Marian smiled at them both. "Good luck." The door closed quietly.

Drake seated Callista at the green baize–covered table. His breath warmed her nape as he said, "Though, I must admit, you most delight me as you were when I first saw you."

Callista's wrist paused, then moved more furiously. Let him tease. He was not likely to see her in dishabille again. She refused to be discomposed. She was a woman of the world tonight, and she had an intimation that, before the clock struck on a new day, she'd feel every one of her two and twenty years.

She snapped the fan closed and set it aside. "Shall we begin?"

"Certainly." He sat down opposite her, the delicate chair creaking slightly under his weight. "We obviously need not assign a value to each point, given the fact that the stakes are already known. Shall we say whoever has the most points after six hands triumphs?"

"Agreed."

"Good. I shall be happy for you to deal first."

Callista nodded regally. "Thank you."

The dealer in piquet always had the advantage because the opponent had to declare first. Callista shuffled and dealt the thirty-two-card deck with an adeptness that made Drake's eyes narrow, but he merely fanned his twelve cards out without comment. His hands were so large that he held the cards with some dexterity despite his missing fingers. His adroitness made her deduce that the injury had occurred long ago. From the screen of her lashes, Callista observed that he rearranged only three of his cards.

She felt a stab of dismay at his obvious experience,

Colleen Shannon

for in piquet, with only eight cards remaining in the deck and the hands declared, then played in tricks, it was not difficult to make an informed guess as to an opponent's hand. For this reason, Callista, too, put only her sets together, leaving the suits where they were dealt.

Fiercely she stared at her cards. Not a good beginning. She had three jacks, two queens, and the ace of hearts, the remaining six cards being eight, nine, or ten. She did, however, have three numbered hearts in a sequence.

Drake discarded only three cards instead of the five allowable, another bad sign. Callista discarded all but the face cards and the run. She drew an ace, the last jack, and, amazingly enough, a ten, a queen, and a king of hearts. She barely restrained a smile. A run of seven cards in one suit was unusual.

Drake declared "sequence and set" confidently, meaning he believed he had a winning sequence in one suit and a winning set.

Callista paused as if hesitant, but inwardly she was elated. Given the fact that she had at least one of every type of card but seven, his set must be in sevens. Her jacks would win. When those slanting dragon eyes glittered in her direction, she said, "Point and sequence. Seven hearts."

"Indeed?" He fanned his cards out further. "Well, I only have six clubs, so the sequence is yours. This time. Set?"

"Four jacks."

"I have four sevens, so the points and sequence are both yours." Calmly she declared her number of points, trying to be gracious when he had nothing to declare. He wrote her score on the piece of paper beside his elbow; then they played the tricks.

These he won, given the fact that he had more face cards, but Callista was still far ahead at the end of the hand.

He stacked the cards neatly and shuffled them mainly with one hand, using his injured hand mostly as a brace, but somehow he made the movement look easy. "You play quite well. For a woman."

"And so do you. For a man."

He smiled faintly. "You let no one get the best of you, do you?"

"No one." She met his shadowy eye slits levelly.

"You know the old saying: 'Pride goeth before a fall.'"

"Indeed. I, too, am familiar with Scriptures. Do you recall 'Oh, how the mighty are fallen?'"

His fingers paused in smoothing the edges of the cards; then he began to deal. "How edifying that you find me mighty."

"Mighty irritating," she muttered.

"What?"

Callista spread her cards before her like a shield, refusing to spar with him verbally any longer. His attempt to make her angry would not work. She told herself that repeatedly over the next three hands, which he won. Her lead shrank and then disappeared as he eked out a four-point lead.

On the fifth hand, her hopes rose. She dealt herself four aces, three jacks, and three tens. If she were lucky in her drawing she could put the match out of his reach. . . .

"Carte blanche," that deep voice said smoothly.

Oh no! That meant he had no face cards and won ten points immediately, even before the discards. She looked at him, wishing for the dozenth time that she could see the man behind the mask.

He stared back, and she had the disconcerting feeling he could read her mind. She dismissed the rude temptation to challenge him, for she was not vindictive. Besides, however vast his flaws, she did not think he would cheat. She nodded and waited for him to discard.

He did so, picking up five cards.

Good. That was the disadvantage of a carte blanche. Even though it offered an immediate score, it often left one little maneuvering room in the balance of the game.

She drew two cards. To her delight, she added a jack and a ten.

Since she had dealt, he declared first. "Point and sequence. Five spades."

"Oh, dear. Twenty-five points for you already."

His mask could not disguise his air of satisfaction—or his dismay when she said sweetly, "Three sets of four. Forty-two points to me."

His mouth tightened, but he added the scores to the sheet without comment. He led with a low spade, which she took with her jack. She made full use of her aces, but he had enough cards in each suit to protect his kings and queens. At the end of the hand, he had seven tricks, which brought his total score for the hand to forty-two. She'd won four tricks with her aces and one other, which brought her total score to forty-seven. She now led by one point.

They were closely matched indeed. Somehow she knew he shared the thought even before he spoke.

"Impasse," he said softly, looking up from the jewel-toned cards staining the table. "This often happens when two equally forceful opponents meet."

The temptation was irresistible. "Didn't you know, sir, as our late genius would say—'To every action

72

there is always opposed an equal reaction.' " There, how was that for a polite snub?

Insufficient, she learned readily enough.

In the act of scooping up the cards, his hands went still. "Are you a student of Newton, then?"

"I'm a student of anything that enriches my mind and thus enhances my existence."

"By Jove, I believe you are."

She was not flattered at the amazement in his voice, and was even less flattered when he continued, "Truly, though, you should finish the quote."

She tried to snap the fan open, but his uninjured hand covered her own. He drawled, " 'The mutual actions of two bodies upon each other are always equal, and directed to contrary parts.' "

She felt more than saw the eyes that delved into her bodice. She didn't help matters by taking a big breath for control. His intensity became almost tangible. Damn, she'd forgotten about the ruffle. She pulled her hand from under his. "Indeed, a body can be most contrary when faced by importuning males. Shall we go on with the game?"

"Why, we have never stopped, my dear. Didn't you know?"

Callista caught herself before she took another deep breath. Rather than choke on frustration, she tapped her toes against the thick rug. When she was calm again, she intoned, "Deal, please."

The high stakes version of piquet they were playing had the nickname Rubicon. As she fanned open that last fateful hand, Callista decided never was a game named so appropriately or fought so hard. No piles of guineas, pound notes, or even IOUs littered the table, but given the cost of Paris and the estate, not to mention the five thousand pounds, Callista could hear the waters rushing under her feet.

Like Caesar, she'd either cross the Rubicon and go on to conquest or drown; she most assuredly could not turn back. She blinked and focused on her cards.

She had four hearts, out of sequence by one, two tens, two queens, an eight, a nine, and two aces. She decided to gamble and discard the tens along with the other numbered cards. If out of the four she drew she snagged the right heart, she'd have a sequence of five, plus five hearts, an excellent opening score. She picked the cards from the stock, inserting each one slowly in her hand.

Her heart sank. She didn't draw the missing card. Still, she drew a queen and an ace, a winning set unless he had kings and jacks, in which case they'd be at a draw. She also drew enough of the other suits to protect her queens. Perhaps the four hearts and two sets would be enough to take the declarations. Judging from the spread, his hand couldn't be much better. She hesitated, but he was waiting.

"Four points and two sets of three," she declared.

His big hand gripped his cards tightly. "How high are your sets?"

"Aces and queens."

The mask fixated on her abruptly. Those delicious masculine lips quivered, but he said solemnly, "Sequence of four and two sets of three." He waited, making her squirm in her seat, before he finally purred, "Kings and jacks."

His tone was as luxurious as a scented bath, but too much was at stake for Callista to bathe in it. "A tie, it would seem," she said coldly.

"So far." His smile widened.

Not for long, she vowed. She slapped one of her aces down. She won all three aces, of course, but since the

74

cards were evenly distributed, he won all three kings plus one ace he'd apparently drawn. He was up by one, which made their total score dead even.

She swallowed, trying to wet her dry throat, wishing she'd accepted Marian's offer of a glass of ratafia. Her forehead, in contrast, was beaded with sweat. She pulled a lace handkerchief from her sleeve and wiped her brow. It was her lead.

"Hot, my dear? Or nervous?"

She shot him a glare. "I am a trifle warm, but since we are almost finished—"

"Are we?"

A big, gloved hand pushed a tendril of hair away from her flushed cheek with a tenderness she longed to believe in—but didn't. "I shall survive."

That whimsical mask tilted as he studied her. "A woman of your wit and beauty is destined for more than mere survival. Don't you want to live up to the promise of that glorious, flaming hair?" He set his cards down and reached out again.

She jerked her head away. "I shall do so as long as I live on my own terms." She slapped down a queen, which was the highest remaining card in the suit. She took that one, only to lose her ten to his jack.

And so it went until Callista had a single card in her hand—a heart. It was her lead, and she'd had more hearts. Unless she'd miscalculated, she'd take the trick, which brought her total to six. She tossed the ten of hearts on the table; he smiled ruefully and ceded his seven of clubs.

Each glanced at the tricks pyramided on opposing sides.

Six apiece.

"Another draw."

Callista's heart lurched before she remembered. A

Colleen Shannon

smile tickled the corners of her lush mouth, then spread over her countenance. "Not quite. I took the last trick, remember? For that, I get a point." Her eyes lifted to his.

He reared back as if startled; then he shook his head like a weary dragon bearded in his lair. "Damn, you're right. I forgot." He tallied the scores carefully again; then he shoved the paper aside. "You win. By one bloody point."

His growl soothed her battered ego enough for her to be gracious. "Would you care for refreshment now?" For the first time that night, her smile was genuine.

That grim attention lifted from the score sheet to her face. She sensed the slide of his gaze from her mouth to her black ruffle. "Yes, but what I thirst for does not, I fear, sit on that sideboard."

The double entendres they'd been exchanging like duelists' shots had finally taken their toll on her nerves. Her ears were ringing from the contest, and for the moment a perky reply was beyond her. Instead she studied him, wondering what had made this man so fierce and so competitive. He stared back, but that blasted mask offered few clues to his thoughts, much less his feelings.

The flames leaped high as a log fell in the fireplace, breaking the spell of his enigmatic gaze. Wearily Callista rose, rubbing her aching temples.

She heard the clatter of bottle against glass. A brandy snifter was thrust into her hand. She wrinkled her nose, but wet her lips before she set the glass down. "Thank you."

A discreet tap sounded at the door; Marian peeked around one of the heavy portals. "Are you finished? Who won?"

The Gentle Beast

"I did. Of course." Callista fanned herself languidly, feeling more the thing.

Marian grinned before her hostess duties reminded her that she should commiserate with her losing guest. She shoved the door wide and entered. "Callista has a near perfect memory."

The ghost of a startled laugh shook that imposing frame. "So do I, madam. So do I." Abruptly he took Callista's hand and kissed it.

The warmth of his mouth climbed up her arm in a wave that singed her cheeks. Her hand tingled so that she barely restrained herself from jerking away.

"A most elucidating evening, my lady. I shall look forward to another, ah, encounter, soon. I will have my barrister draw a check on my account and send it and the deed to you tomorrow. Where should I have them sent?"

Callista hesitated, but Marian tripped over daintily and took her friend's arm. "Here, of course."

Callista was too weary to argue.

Drake also bowed over Marian's hand. "Thank you for your hospitality."

"You are welcome anytime, sir."

He made a sound that might have been doubt or pleasure, nodded to them both, and then strode to the door, leaving it slightly ajar.

They both heard Colter say in chilly tones, "Good evening, sir." The disapproving butler closed the exterior door with a snap.

Callista was touched at his obvious loyalty to her, but her knees still wilted as that brooding presence was withdrawn. The room took on proper proportions again. She collapsed on the settee, wiping her sweating forehead.

"Well! I wish I'd been able to stay." Marian snatched

the fan from Callista's limp hand and waved it before her own face. "I declare, the heat in this room owes little to the fire."

Callista didn't bother denying the obvious. "Where is Henry?"

"Not back yet."

The front door banged open. Simon's exuberant voice called out, "'Lista? Where are you?"

Callista pushed her weary body erect. As she did so, the clock chimed midnight. "Here I am," she called.

"Who was that in the black carriage?" Henry asked, shoving open the door.

Callista hesitated, then admitted, "Drake Herrick."

Henry flinched as if struck. Mildly he asked, "And what, pray, was he doing here?"

Callista was not fooled by his tone. "Being fleeced."

Henry's stillness grew more ominous. "I told you to have nothing to do with him. He is dangerous, especially to you."

"He went away the loser this time."

Henry still looked furious, so it was Simon who asked eagerly, "What did you win?"

"Not much." Callista covered a yawn with her hand. "Only the deed to Summerlea and five thousand pounds."

Simon's shout of triumph echoed three stories high, almost loud enough to burst the windows.

Henry smiled weakly and sought a chair. "I don't know whether to kiss you or spank you. He will be out for blood now."

"A simple thank-you will suffice."

He blew her a kiss. "I am proud of you. You are a fitting heir to Sir Walter Raleigh. The five thousand pounds should be a sufficient deposit. Quartermain likes the house. We'll close the deal tomorrow."

The Gentle Beast

*   *   *

Callista basked in her triumph for a whole week before her world went to pieces. . . .

Part of Summerlea's aged roof caved in, proof, if any was needed, that the five thousand would not run Summerlea for long. Thus the gaming hell was their best chance of raising ready cash. Callista quelled her distaste at being forced to work with Quartermain and labored feverishly in the town house while Henry attended the closing.

She was in the study, shaking out yet another dustcover to see what treasures it hid, when the front door opened. Two sets of agitated steps rushed across the parquet entry.

Callista shoved back a loose strand of hair and hurried out in time to abort Simon's mad rush up the stairs. "What is it?"

Henry was pale. She hurried forward to take his arm and force him to a seat in the study. He hung his head in his hands. "Damn Quartermain. The ruthless bastard."

Callista knelt before him, her heart thudding against her ribs. "What's amiss?"

"Behind my back, he told the barrister we would pay cash for the house and has already paid for his portion. We have to raise another seven thousand or lose the five, which I put down earlier in the week. We will have no quarter interest in the hell if we do not put down the additional capital."

Callista covered her mouth with her hand, but a weak cry of dismay escaped. "I knew we could not trust him."

Simon was striding up and down the room as if he couldn't be still. "I don't believe it," he said repeatedly to his feet. "He's my friend."

Colleen Shannon

Callista surged to her feet. "He does not know the meaning of the word. What now?"

Henry lifted his head and cupped his palm around the diamond casting yellow fire at his throat. "If we sell this and your emerald, we should raise part of it. What about . . ."

Callista shook her head adamantly before he could even suggest it. "No. Never again will I mortgage Summerlea. If all else fails, at least we have somewhere to live."

"To fall about our ears, you mean," Simon grumbled.

"And whose fault is that, pray tell? You should pick your friends with more care."

They glared at one another out of identical green eyes.

Henry rose with weary authority. "Let me speak to my cronies at White's. I may be able to call in some favors." His footsteps dragged as he went back to the entry. "Come along, children."

"You could sell Paris," Simon reminded her as they left the study. "You'll be too busy at the tables to have time to train him now."

Callista opened her mouth to retort, but her toe caught on a loose piece of parquet. Simon grabbed her waist and kept her from falling. She squeezed his arm. "This arguing is useless. Somehow we shall contrive. We always have." It did not occur to her until too late that she had not denied the possibility of selling Paris.

By the time, several days later, she had her first chance to ride Paris in between trips to London, she found his stall empty. She borrowed a neighbor's mare and spanned the road to London in record time, but she was too late. When Simon finally appeared that night at Marian's, he was drunk on equal portions of victory and port.

When he only whistled tunelessly in response to her query, she caught his arms and shook him. "Where did you take him, Simon? Answer me!"

"Lish, uh, Lip . . ."

Callista released him so fast he swayed. "Listing's Livery?" The stable was rapidly gaining a reputation as the best purveyor of horseflesh in the city. They often held private auctions. "Has Paris been sold yet?" *Please, no.* Paris was more than a horse to her. He was a remnant of her happy childhood, as much, if not more, of her legacy than Summerlea.

Simon patted his pocket.

At the crackle, Callista drew out the bank draft. Four thousand pounds. She closed her eyes, but she'd seen the signature once before. That dark scrawl was as bold and black hearted as its author. She opened her eyes.

Drake Herrick.

Damn him. He could afford any racehorse in England, even Eclipse himself. But it was Paris he wanted for one simple reason: she and Henry valued the horse more as a member of the family than as a steed. One by one, he was buying the few things she valued. But Paris, she vowed, would not feel his weight any more than she would. Callista bolted up the stairs and grabbed her mantelet, sticking the draft inside her reticule.

Marian met her at the foot of the landing, on her way to supporting a whistling Simon to the salon. "Where are you going so late?"

"Never mind. I may be late." She hurried out. She didn't have long to wait on the fashionable street before a sedan chair drew near. "New Bond Street. Herrick, Limited." She accepted the bearer's hand into the sedan.

If her luck held, Herrick would agree to another game. If it didn't, she had only Summerlea and herself to barter with.

She knew which stakes he'd demand.

The real choice was—which was more important to her? Her virtue, which would be questioned the second she reigned over London's newest gaming hell, or Paris?

Alone in the dark, she remembered the strength and breeding in every line of Drake's body, and the exquisite skill of his mouth. He had some strange magnetism that superceded fear and distrust. Her own honesty was a limp bulwark against his powerful masculinity.

Yet she didn't order the chair about. No matter how her conscience railed at her in concert with the cobblestones clattering beneath their passage, Callista knew that part of her, at least, longed for the worst fate that could befall her.

Or would it be the best?

Chapter Four

Forlornly Callista watched the sedan chairmen walk away, leaving her alone before a building that glowed faintly on the top floor.

Had she been right to send them away? If she couldn't get in, she'd have to walk several streets over to find another chair. *Needs must* should be her family motto, she thought wryly. One way or another she had to find Herrick tonight. Instinctively she knew he lived near his shop. Every self-respecting dragon guarded his golden hoard.

Drawing her cloak tightly about her body, she took a deep breath and climbed the steps to the shop door.

She rapped the knocker, listening to the faint echo. She waited, glancing uneasily over her shoulder at approaching footsteps. Two burly men rounded the corner, pausing midstep as they saw her. Callista quickly looked back around, pretending to ignore them, but every nerve quivered.

Colleen Shannon

"Blimey, luv, I'd not leave ye standin' at me door."
The lead man hurried forward, his ugly face and broken nose illuminated by the lantern burning by the door.

Callista affected deafness, rapping the knocker so hard her hand ached. Nothing. He was two steps away now. She turned, cornered, and opened her mouth to scream when an older man rushed out of the darkness, brandishing a walking cane.

"Here now, you blighters, don't you know a lady when you see one?" The large, portly man limped slightly, and he trembled with an odd palsy, but he seemed fearless as he stepped between Callista and the two louts.

She thought the prominent nose, full, pouting lips, and slashing eyebrows seemed vaguely familiar, but she was too grateful for his intervention to quibble over his identity.

"I knows a busybody when I sees one, right eno'," growled the taller of the two, doubling up his fists.

To Callista's horror, she heard the scrape of steel. The elderly gentleman now held a long, thin blade, pulled from his cane. In the light by the door, the older man's expression chilled her, but it apparently had little effect on the other two.

One brandished a knife; the other pulled a pistol from his coat.

Unable to stand helplessly by, Callista grabbed the cane the older man had dropped and brandished it. He turned his head, surprised, but she saw the approving gleam in his eyes as he, too, held his sword in the ready position. To free her hands, Callista flung her reticule aside. It hit the door. Callista felt the draft of air and watched, astounded, as the door eased open.

Callista tossed the cane inside, grabbed the man's

84

coat with both hands, and pulled him into the comforting darkness. He made a growl of protest, but she quickly slammed and latched the door.

Just in time, for a bullet pounded the thick wood, raising an evil pockmark on their side of the portal. They listened to the footsteps fading away. The gentleman fumbled for the usual tinderbox beside the door, found one, and lit the lantern on the inside table. In the flickering glow, they stared at one another.

"My dear child, why in the deuce were you loitering about outside when your intended destination was apparently open in anticipation of your arrival?"

Callista's mouth dropped open. No. It was absolutely impossible for Herrick to know she was coming. Why, she hadn't known herself until an hour ago. Callista looked at the imposing old gent, and suddenly she remembered where she'd seen him. All England had seen his likeness in one form or another. Only one man could cut to the heart of a matter so succinctly. The palsy he'd contracted as a baby from a wet nurse might affect his motions; that magnificent wit was not impaired in the slightest.

Callista bent deep in a curtsy. "My dear Dr. Johnson, I am honored to meet you at last. May I be so bold as to say that I am a great admirer of yours?"

Dr. Samuel Johnson bowed. "The admiration is mutual. Why, I cannot think of another living female who'd stand so firmly by my side at such a perilous moment." His face was briefly melancholy.

Callista wondered if he still missed his late wife, Tetty, gone these many years, but he soon shook off whatever thoughts made him sad and looked about curiously at his current surroundings. His face lit up like a child's at a confectionery. "So, this is the infamous Drake Herrick's shop."

Colleen Shannon

"You know him, sir?"

Johnson smiled. "Slightly. I confess we have attended some of the same card parties, though I am not a gamester myself. I declare I'd give a monkey to see what lies behind those cursed masks he wears."

Something else we have in common, Callista thought, *aside from a love of literature.* "So would half of London, no doubt."

"No doubt. If you'll forgive my forwardness—what brings you here so late, my child?"

Callista worried at her reticule, considering a lie, but he was too astute. "He has something of mine. I intend to ask for it back."

Both eyebrows went up, but he was too well bred to press her further. Callista remembered a line from *The Rambler:* "Curiosity is one of the most permanent and certain characteristics of a vigorous intellect."

The author, who so richly fit his own writings, snapped open his pocket watch and harrumphed. "Yes, well, I see."

No doubt he did. Callista squirmed inside, but remained calm outwardly.

"But since I am already late for an engagement, please forgive my hasty departure." He put his hand on the latch, then glanced at her. "It's none of my business, of course, but are you sure this cannot wait until the morn? Herrick is not . . . suitable company for a gently bred female."

Callista had to smile. "Ah, many would say that I am neither gentle nor well bred."

An appreciative gaze went over her. "Forsooth, I challenge anyone to deny you are female. Good luck, my child. I hope we meet again." He winked and was gone.

Callista's smile was slow to fade. She'd always

The Gentle Beast

longed to meet Johnson. In truth, it was a rare man whose nature lived up to his reputation.

The thought made her think of the man awaiting her. His reputation was far less savory than Johnson's. Callista glanced up the stairs, frowning now. She patted her reticule, hearing the rattle of the bank note. It reminded her of why she'd come and of what she sought. Resolutely she approached the staircase that, in the darkness, seemed to stretch like the road to Golgotha.

She squashed the longing for her own safe bed, instead marching up the carpeted stairs toward that telltale light. Lit wall sconces lined the way, leading her deeper into the dragon's lair. At the corner, near his office, the lights were snuffed. When she peeked inside she saw a single lantern burning on his desk. A muted glow beckoned far away down the secret passageway steps, the door to which just happened to be open.

A trail of bank notes could hardly have been more obvious. But the symbolism of the lights was not lost on her. Flame to the moth. And she was as surely drawn, as likely to be burned.

Callista leaned against the wall, wondering if she dared accept the invitation. She closed her eyes and pictured Paris, whickering in welcome as she brought him sugar.

Before she could change her mind, she caught the reticule close to her side and began the long descent into the Dragon's realm. . . .

Henry stared at Marian. "What the devil do you mean you don't know where she is?"

Marian twisted her delicate lace handkerchief so hard that it tore. "I only know she said she'd be late. One of my footmen said she took a sedan chair."

"Well, question the damned fellow."

Colleen Shannon

"My man has not been able to find him. He must have retired for the night."

Henry checked his pocket watch for the third time. "Deuce take it, woman, why in God's name did you not stop her? She's gone to *him!*"

Abruptly Marian shoved her handkerchief up her wrapper sleeve. "I make no doubt that our docile, obedient Callista always does exactly as you tell her."

Henry sighed at the sarcasm and jammed his watch back into his waistcoat. "Of course you are right. Forgive me, child. I am not myself." His hand went to his snowy neckcloth.

Marian watched the movement, expecting to see that familiar glitter of yellow. Her eyes bugged out. The Yellow Rose was gone! "Oh, Henry, you didn't sell your stickpin. . . ."

His hand dropped. "No mere possession is worth a moment of Callista's happiness. I lost her fortune. I am honor-bound to help her recover it."

Henry kicked his son's feet. Simon started groggily up from his sprawling position in a comfortable chair, and then grabbed his head. "Fiend seize it, do not accost me or my head will fall off!"

"So? Since you seldom use it for aught but a hat rack, 'tis no great loss."

Simon glared.

Henry glared right back, the hectic flush in his cheeks hinting of the handsome buck he had once been. "Get up. We're off to Herrick's shop. Callista must be there."

Marian watched Simon struggle into his greatcoat. "Henry, when will you tell us why Herrick hates you so?"

"I swear I am not certain, Marian. Unless . . ."

"Unless?"

The Gentle Beast

"He sometimes reminds me of someone I used to know. Come along, Simon." Henry grabbed his son's arm and dragged him to the door.

Marian jumped as the great front door closed with a bang. She glanced up the stairs, but she knew she'd only toss and turn if she tried to go to bed. Instead she went into the drawing room, planted two lanterns next to her favorite settee, and pulled up her embroidery frame. The passive activity was little distraction.

Far better than Henry, she realized that Callista's real danger lay not in Herrick himself, but in her friend's own attraction to him. The air had been so charged between the pair that night they gambled that Marian's very hair had stood on end. Furthermore, despite Herrick's fearsome reputation, he was basically a gentleman. Marian would stake all she owned on that.

How would Callista react when that potent masculinity tantalized her? Would she be strong enough to resist?

More to the point—would she want to?

A short distance away, Callista was indeed mesmerized. She stood in a wonderland so lovely she could scarce grasp it. The stairs had seemed endless, but the muted light had become a blaze as she exited the narrow stairwell. Her feet sank into carpet so plush her soft slippers left imprints. She looked down and gasped.

An oriental carpet covered a vast room from wall to wall, its design so intricate and colorful that it was sacrilege to walk on it. Even Marian didn't own one so fine. The room blazed with light from the dozens of Austrian crystal chandeliers winking far above her head. Callista spied lacy ironwork making a catwalk above her. The walk led to a raised platform lined with

89

vivid carmine drapes drawn about a large object she couldn't make out.

Callista stepped forward hesitantly. Whatever else Herrick was, he had a taste for beautiful things. The walls were covered in an expensive French wallpaper embossed with yellow roses. At another time, she might have frowned at their significance, but she was too busy staring at the artwork. A Rembrandt, a Reynolds, even, no, it couldn't be . . . a da Vinci?

An ermine fur rug sat in front of an exquisite divan next to a roaring fire. Another fur, this one dark and shining, lay at the foot of the divan, ready, ludicrously enough, to be a leg warmer.

Inlaid tables held marble, ivory, and jade figurines both sublime and nonsensical, from nymphs and satyrs to dragons and ships.

Callista passed an open chest brimming with black and pink pearls. She pulled out a necklace so long that it fell to her knees when she hesitantly tried it on. She quickly pulled it off and put it back, closing off the chest—and temptation. It hadn't escaped her that the brilliant light was centered on the middle of the room. The rear was in shadows, but she felt watching eyes.

He was waiting for her.

She knew her myths. Nothing infuriated a dragon more than to be stolen from. She wandered the room, allowing him his little charade. Let him watch. Like Athena, she could be both bright eyed and vigilant. As to the wisdom of her presence here, well, that remained to be seen.

She paused at a table spread with an exquisite chess set. The board was ebony and mother-of-pearl. The white pieces were ivory, carved to resemble actual historical figures of England. The queen had the long nose of Elizabeth; the king was portly, like Henry VIII. She recognized her own beloved ancestor, Sir Walter Raleigh, as one of the knights. Another looked like all the images she'd seen of St. George.

The black pieces, on the other hand, were smooth and luminescent. They reflected the lights as she turned them this way and that. The king and queen were dragons, their pawns gnomes, their bishops winged griffins. The figures were creatures of the night, both horrible and magnetic.

Like their owner.

The mythical against the real. For a moment Callista was chilled, for the analogy of her ancestor risking all to defeat a beastly dragon king was no coincidence. Had Herrick imported this terrible treasure just for her? As though she needed reminding of what was at stake . . .

"Would you like to play?" said that deep voice from over her shoulder.

Another double entendre, no doubt, but Callista was in no mood for it. "I had a different game in mind."

"Pity. Don't you want to know where I got the set?"

"Hardly. I'm afraid to ask."

"I bought it from a carver in the colonies. The black rock is found there and is a form of hematite."

Finally Callista turned to him. His mask this time was black. His tall form was hugged from head to foot by a black silk shirt and black leather trousers that showed his virility in a most explicit way. Black pigskin boots molded his calves.

Callista's heart pounded a warning, but she forced herself to hold the gaze glittering with an intent she'd have given her right arm to read. "Oh, yes? And here I thought you had conjured it from the nether regions yourself."

Laughter shook that imposing frame. "That is what

I most admire in you, my dear. Afraid you might be, but I shall be damned to hell before you show it." He took a step nearer. "But then, with the proper company, even that journey could be enjoyable. As I recall, Persephone learned to relish her four months of darkness and to care for her king of night."

"Ah, but she had the light to look forward to, and only her body was imprisoned. You, sir, are ever night, for your darkness you carry with you." Callista had to stop herself from recoiling, so quickly did his genial attitude change to dangerous stillness.

"How acute you are. In that way you take after your stepfather. At times I almost let myself forget that." He stared another moment longer; then, with a little shake of his head, he strode past her to a sideboard and poured them each a snifter of brandy. He handed her one, swirling his own and inhaling the fine aroma.

She realized she should be insulted that he was offering a lady such strong spirits, but never had she needed a reviving drink more. She tossed back her head and swallowed it all in one draft. And almost collapsed where she stood as fire gushed from her belly to her toes, licking at her very fingertips.

He caught the delicate crystal glass before she dropped it. "I didn't realize you had such appetites."

"You . . . d-don't . . . realize much about m-me," she gasped, tears in her eyes. "Don't give me a challenge unless you want me to meet it."

Those decidedly male lips quirked. He set the glasses aside and approached. Somehow she stood her ground. He leaned so close that his breath, like a dragon's, singed her cheeks. He smelled of brandy, and man, and forgetfulness, but ten generations of Raleighs stiffened her spine.

"I challenge you, then, to defy the conventions you

claim to despise and to become my lady."

She stared into those glittering eye slits. *No, surely even he wouldn't suggest* . . . "Are you proposing to me, sir?"

His head reared back. The mask slipped, but he caught it and tied it firmly behind his head. "No. There will be no lies between us." That gorgeous mouth turned down. "At least, no more than usual. I want you in every way a man wants a woman, and in return I shall shower you with jewels, gowns, carriages. I'll fix Summerlea. I'll set your stepfather and brother up in their hell, so that bastard Quartermain has no interest."

"With yourself in his stead?" Callista picked up a chess piece and pretended intense curiosity, for she couldn't dare let him see the tears misting her eyes. Fiercely she bit them back. He would never know how he'd hurt her. Perhaps her reputation left a bit to be desired, but this was a cut direct. "You'll forgive me, sir, but given your past behavior, I find your generosity a bit . . . suspicious."

"You can't credit me with a change of heart?"

"No. I confess I've sometimes doubted you have one. I've never known a dragon before, you see." There, that was the trick. Pretend a lightness she didn't feel. She carefully set the chess piece down to avoid throwing it at him.

He spanned the remaining gap between them, picked up her hand, and pulled off her glove. He kissed her wrist at the pulse point, unbuttoned his silk shirt, and pulled her hand inside.

Callista gasped. Her fingers curled at the feel of him—soft hair covering vital, warm flesh. She felt the flexing power of his muscles, and, beneath that, a beating heart that signified his humanity. She tried to pull away, but he forced her hand flat, rubbing it around and sighing in pleasure at her touch.

"See?" he whispered. "Everything is very simple, when we allow it to be so. I felt your heart surge under my mouth. And you can't deny that my own resounds to your touch. I am but man. You are but woman. Can we not begin anew on that basis?"

"Then you give up your vengeance against Henry?"

She felt his abrupt tension. She didn't know whether to be glad or sad when he pulled her hand away. In another reality, she might have been pleased at the obvious effort he spent, but in this fantastic world of brilliant light and stygian night, where myth and reality collided, right wore the wrong face. She couldn't trust him, or anything about him.

Much less her own reactions.

Abruptly she turned away, fighting tears again. What had possessed her to come here? She bit back a bitter laugh. He had. And he would possess her fully, in every sense of the word, if she didn't get the hell out of here.

"Thank you for the offer, sir, but you don't have anything I want." She picked up her reticule and turned toward the door. She would deposit the bank note forthwith. Never would she humiliate herself to this man further by begging him for a morsel of kindness he obviously did not possess.

"Not even Paris?"

She stopped cold. And coldly turned back toward him. "Ah, so we get to the meat of the matter at last. You bought him solely to get me here. That's why you left everything open, that's why—" She squelched harsher words that would have told him of her near brush with disaster outside without the timely intervention of Dr. Johnson.

Her safety and her happiness were of supreme indifference to him. Despite all his pretty words she was but a tool to get to Henry.

"I knew you would come, yes. But I own I also hoped you would. You intended to propose another card match, I imagine. I reciprocate with a more appropriate one. If you were mine, we would jointly own Paris, and could train him together."

"Keep him. I will love him and miss him to my dying day, but I'll be no man's possession, least of all in a ploy to harm the only father I have ever known." Her voice broke before she could control it, and she fled for the door.

In one swoop he was on her. Perhaps it was the fanciful setting, but she swore she heard the beat of dragon wings, and his talons seemed to bite as he caught her wrist. She struggled, but she was drawn inexorably closer. She turned her head aside, expecting the blast of his anger, but his voice was even more dangerous.

It came in a seductive whisper. "I thought you more honest with yourself than that, my love. You don't leave in high dudgeon; you flee. Well, before I let you go, you must admit one thing." He hauled her so close that she matched him, length for length.

The closeness accentuated the differences between them: curves against lines, softness meeting hardness. His voice became a veritable purr. "I have something that you want very badly, though you may not know it yet."

Let me go, let me go, her nerves screamed, but a deeper, darker side to her nature wanted to rub against him and savor those dangerous differences. She had to clear her husky voice. "And what, pray, is that?"

The Dragon swooped. And with the first touch of his lips, Callista felt fire engulf her. At first she lay helpless in his clutches, her senses reeling. His lips were so mobile, so warm, moving upon hers, yet gentle withal. *Ask, and ye shall receive. Seek, and ye shall find.*

The blasphemous thoughts burned to ashes under the fire of his kiss. His tongue quested, then gained entrance. He pulled her closer, and she felt a strange hardness pressing into her abdomen. It called to her in some way she couldn't fathom, creating a weakness in her lower limbs. The flames spread outward from her lips, eating at her very vitals, down to the tips of her toes. She was being consumed, yet it wasn't enough. Something was missing. With a small sound of greed she didn't even know she made, she pressed her hands inside his shirt and caressed the reality of skin and bone. Masks the beast might wear, but at this moment he had never been more vitally male.

And he called to all that was female in her. She felt his breath catch. Then the trail of fire followed his lips down her arched neck to the opening of her bodice. Her heart leaped to his mouth. As if, in some strange way, it belonged to him.

Her eyelashes fluttered as she felt his hands at her stays, where no man had ever touched, but protest was beyond her. He was right, damn him. This, she did want. No man's lips had ever made her seek the night and all its gifts. . . .

"Excuse me, sir, but you've a guest upstairs."

The strong hands withdrew. Drake caught her about the waist to help her gain her feet. She made a little sound of protest, but reluctantly opened her eyes. The realm of fire and darkness was gone. Reality was firmly beneath her feet. And, despite the riches in the room, she felt the poorer for it. Reality intruded in an even more basic way as she met the manager's eyes.

The Gentle Beast

His disapproval flickered plainly before he looked at his master again. "I tried to send them away, but they demand to see you."

Drake took a couple of deep, calming breaths, tied his hair back in its queue again, and then firmly set Callista on the settee by the fire. "An importunate visitor, my dear. I'll be back in a trice."

His steps retreated up the stairs. The opening swung shut behind him, leaving Callista alone with the crackling fire and her shame.

What had possessed her? The turn of phrase elicited a nervous laugh. Dragon fodder, but for the timely intervention. She buried her hot face in her hands and refastened the top of her stays, which, thank God, was all he'd managed to undo. Then she surged to her feet and ran to the door—which had disappeared. Feel though she did for the telltale crack, the paneling on this side of the wall seemed smooth and unbroken. She twitched at a carved boss, pulled every protuberance, but nothing moved.

She beat on it in frustration. "Help me! Please, is anyone there?"

Nothing. As usual she could rely on no one but herself. She marched back into the treasure vault, seeking . . . what? A weapon? What would she do with it if she found it?

She circled the perimeter, looking for a window. She found three, too high for her to reach and covered with black glaze. From the exterior, this secret chamber would be invisible. He could hold her here at his whim, and no one would ever find her.

Like a dragon's lair. Alarmed at the thought, she looked harder for some means of escape. She felt with her hands along the wall, passed a crack, and went back to it. Her fingers traced the outline of a door. She felt, but couldn't find a knob. She bent down and spied a tiny keyhole.

She looked above the door, beside it, but he wouldn't leave the key so accessible, even if no one else knew about his lair. Her gaze caught the mysterious crimson eminence far above her head. She approached the spiral staircase against the wall and followed the lacy balustrade up and up to the catwalk. She saw a long track suspended from the ceiling and a pull cord. She tugged, and with a whoosh, the expensive red curtains winged aside, revealing a bed, nightstand, and vast armoire.

She gasped. The bed was huge, even for a man of Drake's size. It was marquetry, the exquisite, glossy finish mixing ebony, cherry, and alabaster, each color accenting the lines of a great beast. The immense canopy looked like a dragon's wings, the headboard a dragon's head, with the sides of the bed legs ending in claw footposts. The red silk hangings accented the bold, menacing beauty of it.

"Thank God I don't have to sleep in that thing," she muttered, little knowing she was tempting something even more mystical and problematic: fate.

Feeling more than ever an invader in this fantastic lair—a morsel for the Dragon—she searched the armoire. She found only shirts, coats, and pants of the finest quality. Next she looked in the nightstand, pulling out a small bottle of laudanum, writing parchment, a quill, and ink. On the shelf beneath she found a pamphlet that made her gasp.

All of London was talking about the *Letters of Junius*. The identity of the anonymous rabble-rouser, who was despised by every good Tory and hotly sought for treason by the king, was the latest gossip in the coffeehouses. Many believed the author none other than

The Gentle Beast

John Wilkes, who had thrice been denied his legally elected seat in the House of Commons by the king.

Against Henry's wishes, Callista had attended a meeting of one of the societies that had sprung up to push for parliamentary reform. She found many of the people there too radical, but a few had made sheer common sense. If the House of Commons didn't speak for the people, who did? If the English people could not duly elect their representatives, and were at the mere whim of one man, how could the most enlightened country in the world claim to be any part of the Age of Reason?

Callista set the pamphlet back carefully, not knowing what to think. Callista rose, searching the rest of the odd bedchamber.

She was pushing past the bed, catching a dragon's claw as she rounded it, when she felt the post move. She unscrewed it and looked inside. She pulled out a long, narrow tube with a slit in the side. She poked and a hidden spring lifted up the trap opening. She shook the contents out on the priceless rug beside the bed.

Diamonds, rubies, and emeralds rolled across the rug, sparkling as they moved. Some were as large as plums, others of a clarity so perfect she thought it sacrilege to keep them hidden. Gold coins, some bearing Caesar's image, others from Spain, still others of Arabic origin, weighted one end; good gold English sovereigns the other. A dragon's emergency hoard, she supposed. However, it was the innocuous key among all the other riches that really caught her eye. Putting everything else back, she took the key down to the door with no knob.

It fit perfectly. Taking a sconce of candles with her, she shoved open the door, holding her breath. At first she was almost disappointed. She'd expected some alchemist's shop, she supposed, where this fantastic man derived his wealth. She saw a hulking shape in the corner and went closer.

Why, it was merely a printer's press. Why did Drake have it, and why had he gone to such pains to conceal it? She picked up one of the sheets that were neatly stacked, waiting to be folded.

She gasped and held the candle higher, not believing her eyes. It was the frontispiece for a *Letter of Junius*. And it bore a date two days hence!

My God, what had she stumbled across?

What would he do to her if he found her here?

Drake crossed one long leg over the other, pretending boredom, while his mind—and a rather more southerly part of his anatomy—urged him to return to Callista posthaste. Before she changed her mind, or even found the concealed opening to the stair entrance.

"May you rot in hell, I know you have her!" Henry leaned heavily on his walking stick, his face pasty under the periwig.

Simon watched warily, blinking against the light that obviously hurt his aching head. Clyde sat placidly in a chair against the wall. Only Drake recognized his tension.

"Since you and your son have searched my premises for the past half hour and found nothing," Drake replied, "do you think I've spirited her into the air?"

Henry could only grind his teeth. Drake watched through his mask slits as Henry grasped his cane and began to lift it. *Come on, old man. Give me a reason, do. I'd love to beat you within an inch of the life you took from me. . . .*

Something of his thoughts must have shown in his

posture, for Simon, after a glance at him, stared. He caught Henry's arm, forcing the cane back down. "Come, Father. In the morning we'll bring the watch."

Drake rose, no longer able to affect boredom. "Yes, do. I'll help them search the block, if you so wish."

Henry started for the door, shoving past Clyde. "You've not seen the last of us, you sick bastard. And mark this." In the doorway he turned so fast that Simon bumped into him. "I've powerful friends. Leave me and mine alone, or you shall have more enemies than me to reckon with."

Drake laughed softly. "Quartermain, I deduce. My good man, do you not know I can buy him and sell him several times over?"

Henry and Simon stared. For once Henry seemed speechless.

Simon blustered, "But . . . but . . ."

Drake leaned casually against his desk. "How do I know about your recent alliance, I believe you're trying to ask?"

Simon nodded, but Drake looked only at Henry.

"I've eyes and ears throughout the world, not just London. Information is power, and power is money, my dear old enemy. Had you taken the trouble to learn more about your silent business partner, you'd not be in such dire straits now. Why, I could tell you what our mad King George supped on last night. Two partridges, a brace of . . ."

Eyes popping with fear, Simon dragged Henry out the door.

Drake sat against the desk, chuckling with glee at Henry's last expression.

Clyde watched glumly. "I only hope you get to laugh last, my lord."

Drake stopped laughing and scowled at the only

Colleen Shannon

friend he had. "I have told you not to call me that. I am not ready for anyone to know yet."

"I do not understand all these machinations. Why can you not take your rightful place and repossess without further ado?"

"Because it would not be near as much fun that way." Drake's voice softened to a tone that would have made anyone but Clyde back away. "And because Henry will know penitence before I'm done."

Clyde shook his head. "You are not a priest. 'Tis sacrilege for you to talk that way."

"Perhaps. But vengeance will be no less sweet. Now, my friend, fetch my carriage. As much as I'd like to toy with her longer, I'd best send the little thorn in my garden home. The last thing I need is trouble with the authorities."

"Amen to that," said Clyde with a pious look toward heaven.

"You were born a century too late, you old sourpuss. You should have served Cromwell instead of a libertine like me."

Drake opened the stair door and descended, his soft-soled boots making little sound. He left the panel open, intending to take her straight back up. He sighed with regret. She made him feel alive, as nothing had in a very long time. Even the gaming tables and the stock exchange were beginning to bore him.

She wasn't on the settee, where he'd left her. He spied the red curtains, pulled back, and grinned. Of course, she would have had to explore the rest of his domain. He walked toward the catwalk, his heartbeat accelerating as he envisioned her, white skin gleaming, red hair spread over the bedcovers until he couldn't tell her satin textures from the silk beneath. . . .

The lovely vision was spoiled when he saw the hidden closet panel gaping wide. A muted glow came from inside. His heart lurched, then pounded with a different emotion. He surged forward, slamming the panel back against the wall.

There she stood, her skin luminous in the flattering glow, but the fear on her face banished the last of his dream. The leaflet she held fluttered to the plank floor. He didn't need to look at it to know what it was. She took two steps back, butting up against the press. The candle shook so much he grabbed it before she dropped it.

He'd spent the last twenty years learning to control his emotions, but be damned if she didn't make him feel like a boiling cauldron. Unwelcome feelings roiled within him: anger, disappointment, fear.

And then the lightest feeling boiled to the top—elation. He could keep her now. Not even Clyde could fault him now she'd seen the press.

"Curiosity is a dangerous luxury, puss," he drawled. "I should have tied you to the settee." Holding the candle in one hand, he grabbed her wrist with the other and pulled her outside. She followed obediently, and the unusual behavior made him suspicious. He glanced at her gloved hands, but she held no weapon.

He pushed her down on the settee. She folded her hands in her lap and appraised them.

"Well, what have you to say for yourself, invading my privacy that way?"

It seemed she wouldn't answer at first; then she intoned, "In my darkest moments, I never considered you a traitor."

He stiffened as if she'd punched him. "A traitor to that imported Hanoverian madman, or an Englishman obeying his heart and mind to better the lot of all his countrymen?"

She looked up at him solemnly. "The Jacobites were twice defeated, sir. And George is as much an Englishman as you or I. He was born here, I remind you."

He made a disgusted sound. "Of tainted German blood. He's an obstinate, stupid ruler who has no business being king. He's about to lose us the colonies, and he may face his own little revolution here, if he does not allow his people the right to choose their own representatives."

"So you are a believer in John Wilkes."

"I am a believer in right over wrong, and truth over lies."

She stood. "In that case, you should not object to my leaving."

He blocked her path to the door. "I fear our interpretation of those two verities may differ a trifle. For instance, is it right for me to let you destroy the work of other good Englishmen with more to gain than I?"

"And why do you assume I shall tell the truth about you?"

"You are a woman."

She cocked her head. "Therefore not to be trusted?"

"Not with a secret such as this."

She sat back down and refolded her hands. "Then what do you propose? Would you like to cut out my tongue?" She stuck it out obligingly.

He chuckled. "And deprive myself?"

She blushed and hung her head.

The last of his anger fled on the fleet wings of laughter. When he collected himself, he said, "I was speaking of your wit, though I admit to enjoying your tongue in other, ah . . . areas."

She turned an even deeper hue.

He took mercy on her embarrassment. "Very well, sweet, I'll desist. In this instance. On the other, I must

The Gentle Beast

be firm. You shall be my guest for a while."

Her face took on an obstinate cast. "Your prisoner, you mean."

"If you wish." He was glad of the mask, so she couldn't see how she'd hurt him.

"And if I refuse?"

A log fell in the fire with a crash. She started, but he merely stared at her. "Then it will be a difficult time for us both, but rather harder on you than on me." Devil a bit, but she didn't need to know that.

"And if I stay willingly? Will you leave Henry be?"

It was his turn to hesitate. He considered lying, but something in that clear green gaze dragged the truth from him. "Nothing on this earth can stop the consequences of his own greed. Quartermain has his hooks in him now."

"It's not Quartermain I fear."

He drew in a shocked breath, for fear was the last emotion he wanted to instill in her. For the briefest instant he remembered their first meeting—at least the first since they were grown—and how deliberately he'd tried to frighten her. What had changed since then?

Unwilling to delve into such dangerous emotional waters, he leaned casually against a table. "You have naught to fear from me. I will ask nothing of you that you do not wish to give. My word as an Englishman."

Somehow she didn't look reassured. He could scarce blame her, given their history. She rose and began to wander the vast room, touching a statue here, fondling a table there. It did not escape his notice that her perambulations brought her closer to the door with every step.

"I'll consider it, but for the nonce, do you think you can pour me some more of that delightful brandy?" She fingered a statue of Aphrodite.

Colleen Shannon

He thought how strong the resemblance, but in truth she more fit Athena, goddess of war, in nature. He watched her warily as he approached the sideboard, but she remained contemplative over the statue he'd bought from a Greek fisherman who claimed to have brought it up from a wrecked galleon.

He turned slightly aside to watch what he was doing, so he only saw her movement as a flash from the corner of his eye. He set the decanter down so hastily it toppled, but she still had the door open by the time he started to move. He'd never seen a woman so swift and graceful.

A laugh rumbled in his chest as he leaped after her. By Jove, she made the chase sweet. A conquest easily won was little worth the effort. This vixen would take all his skills before he ran her to ground.

And what then?

She was six steps up when he caught her about the waist. She lashed back at him with feet and fists, but her slippered shoes did no damage, and her fists were tiny compared to those he'd grown up with. He subdued her easily and carried her, kicking, back down the steps, slamming the portal closed with his foot.

"As I said, females are not to be trusted." He tossed her in a chair and imprisoned her by leaning close, grasping each chair arm.

"And you expect me to sit idly by and allow you to practice this . . . perfidy on me?"

"You've been reading too many gothic novels, my sweet. I swear I shall not have my wicked way with you. . . ." He leaned close enough to kiss her ear, finishing softly, ". . . unless, of course, you wish it. I am ever one to please a lady."

She shoved him away and rose, rubbing her elbows, but he'd felt the telltale shiver. He smiled and sat back in the same chair, relishing the warmth she'd left. He flung a long leg over the chair arm and swung it idly as she continued her wanderings. When she came to the chest of pearls, he suggested, "You may have one string of your choosing."

Her hands skittered away. "No, thank you. I have a feeling that it is best not to be indebted to you."

His leg went still. " 'Tis too late for that."

She whirled around, propping her hands on her hips and glaring. "Enough! I am no squeaking little mouse to your tomcat. If I am to give up my freedom, the least you can do is tell me why. We both know the real reason you hold me has little to do with the printing press, and more to do with who my father is."

He lay back, staring at her. She was magnificent, a heady combination of fire and tenderness, intelligence and kindness. She had much of her mother in her. What was it about these Raleigh women? The words were out before he could stop them. "No, my lady. It has most to do with who *you* are."

Her arms dropped as she cocked her head in that curious way he was beginning to recognize.

"What the deuce do you mean by that?"

To distract her, he leaped to his feet. "You'll discover that soon enough. For now, would you care for a light supper?"

"I'm not hungry." She covered a yawn.

"Forgive me. It is late. You know the way to my bed, I believe."

Her hand fell limply to her side. "I will be fine on the settee."

"Nonsense. Come along." He caught her arm. He felt her resistance, but rather than lose in a contest of strength, she bided her time, following along. His respect for her, already high, rose. She was the only woman he'd ever known whose stunning looks matched her character. Like Pallas Athena, she combined wisdom with courage, knowing when to retreat and when to advance.

But times were early. Doubtless she would disappoint, as all women had. He only lusted for her. Once he sated himself in that satin body, this odd obsession would cease.

When they reached the alcove, she jerked her arm away and stood, statuelike, beside the bed. Hiding a smile, he pulled the down comforter back, showing a vast, inviting expanse of snowy linen sheets. He pushed her down and pulled off her slippers, but when his hands went to her bodice, she covered them with her own.

"Please."

"Please . . . what?" In the muted lighting of the lamp beside the bed, they stared at each other. With his hands so intimately positioned, he felt how fast her breathing was. His own accelerated. He wanted nothing so much as to share this vast bed with her and make his vision a reality. As to her feelings—was she aroused or frightened?

Her eyes were a darker green than usual. "Please, you promised to leave me be."

He stood straight, his hands feeling empty with the vital loss of her. "I was merely trying to make you comfortable. Sleep well." *I will not.*

Drawing the drapery about the alcove, he went back down the stairs. With new eyes, he appraised the fantastic abode he'd designed for his own pleasure, a last refuge against the world. In his early days, shortly after his escape, he'd sometimes gone without food to acquire these treasures. But as he looked at the objects from every corner of the globe, acquired in a life of wandering, he wondered if he was right to hoard them.

And, as he listened to the rustling silks above him, an even more alarming thought struck him.

For the first time, his lair felt lonely. . . .

Henry slapped a heavy bag of guineas before Quartermain. "Three thousand on account."

Quartermain opened the bag and began to count.

Henry was furious at the slight, but he was so worried about Callista that he let it pass. He turned to leave.

Without losing count, Quartermain asked, "And where is our fair hostess? We'll have much better business with her as our drawing card."

How the devil did Quartermain know? "I haven't found her yet. But I will." He was on his way to wake the magistrate now, but wanted to give Quartermain the money from the Yellow Rose before Simon got his paws on it.

"I may be able to help, old chap."

Henry stopped at the door, turning to face his partner. If they hadn't already signed the agreement, he'd give the bastard his walking papers, right enough. "I do not want anyone to know she is missing."

"And you trust the magistrates to keep it quiet? Not very wise, I fear."

"What can you do?"

"I? Little. But those who work for me"—Quartermain finished the count and shoved the bag aside—"are, shall we say, eager to do my bidding. If you like, I can have them make discreet inquiries at the warehouse district."

Henry felt like a bug on a pin, held by those ruthless blue eyes. How did he know the Dragon had her? Like calling to like, Henry decided disdainfully, but he nodded cordially enough. "I should be eternally grateful."

Quartermain rose. "And so you shall be, my dear Henry, before we're done." He escorted Henry to the door. "I take it the rest of your share will be shortly forthcoming?"

Henry paused on the stoop. "We're working on it."

"Good. 'Twould be a shame if you lost all you had worked so hard for. Good night. As soon as I hear anything, I will send for you."

Henry left before the door could close in his face. He leaned heavily on his walking stick as he went back to his hired chair, but his face bore the determined expression of the man he used to be.

He was spurred by one thought. Callista's beloved face swam before his eyes. Two of the most powerful men in England wanted her. Neither deserved her.

Somehow he'd defeat them both and keep her safe. If he had to give his own life in the process.

If Drake Herrick was whom he suspected, it could well come to that. . . .

Chapter Five

The smell of tea and scones awoke Callista. Her stomach rumbled with a will of its own, but she was reluctant to lose the lovely dream.

She and her family were enjoying a bucolic picnic, with lambs gamboling in the distance and Summerlea smiling benignly from a rise. Drake's head rested in her lap while their twin sons chased butterflies. Drake's face, unmasked at last, was gentle as he looked up at her. Her heart swelled with love for him.

Where had she seen him before? She was searching a dark, gloomy space for the answer when china clattered as the alcove curtains were whisked aside. The tatters of her dream went with them.

Callista opened her eyes, the last of the warmth dying as yet another dragon mask stared down at her. This one was white, winsome, and unthreatening, but she still hated it. The dream made her bold. She had to see what he looked like. She reached out, but his strong hand caught hers and wrapped her fingers about a china cup handle.

"Good morning, my dear. I have cream and sugar, if you wish it."

She sat up, the covers falling to her waist. "No, I like it plain." She sipped, awakening fully as she felt his gaze burning on her bodice.

What little there was of it.

He drawled, still staring, "Not I. I like my tea . . . full-bodied."

She set the cup down so hastily that tea splashed into the saucer. She tucked the covers about her ample bosom. "I had only my shift to sleep in."

He turned away, but she saw his jaw muscle flex under the mask. "Of course. I have taken the liberty of ordering some clothes for you."

She stared. "Surely they're not ready so soon."

"'Tis amazing what money can do."

"Indeed," Callista agreed coldly. In that area, certainly, she could not compete, but one thing he could not force on her. "You've wasted your ready, I fear. I will not wear them."

He stopped, one hand on the balustrade, and looked over his shoulder. "You shall."

Her mouth tightened. "I am not your kept woman, and I will not be treated as such."

"No, but you shall be pampered as a most favored guest. Which is exactly what you are."

"Pretty words do not dress up an ugly deed. I am not here at will."

He turned and came back, leaning over her. Instinct told her to cower and dive under the covers, but she held her head high and stared directly into those glittering eye slits. Damn him and his masks.

"Yet. Give me a few days."

The Gentle Beast

A shiver crept up Callista's spine. "You may take a year, sir, but a kidnapping is still a kidnapping."

"Oh, yes? The difference 'tween a prison and a home can be summed up in one word." He stayed still, letting her wonder, before he finished huskily, "Love."

Utter silence prevailed. Was this what he offered her? Something in his still, watching posture warned her to be wary. To fall in love with him would be the final humiliation, and would offer him the final victory over her and Henry.

"That, you beast, is something you will never receive from me."

Abruptly he straightened. "Did I ask for it? In truth, love is a burden I long ago learned to do without." An undercurrent in his tone, a tinge of loss or loneliness, made her stare at him.

Then, like a man tossing off a too heavy cape, he shrugged and turned toward the stairs. "I suggest you dress in a day gown or, by my troth, I shall delight in putting you in one myself." Teeth almost as white as the mask flashed in a bold grin. "I have long wanted to discover what treasures you hide under your clothes. We dragons are greedy, you see."

Firm steps receded, leaving her alone with her hopes and fears. And the memory of the desolation in his voice. For the first time she tried to walk in his steps. What terrible trials had forged this man of steel? Yet when he laughed, or kissed her, or saw to her comforts, she glimpsed another side of him, a gentle side she had no defense against.

Callista nibbled on the scone, so lost in her thoughts that she started when someone spoke.

"Good morn', mistress. The master requested that I bring these." The store manager set several large boxes on the locker at the foot of the bed.

Callista blushed and pulled the drooping covers high again. "Thank you."

And be damned to him and the feelings he inspires in me. Callista didn't say it, however. This poor man, disapproving as he obviously was of her, didn't deserve to be dragged into her battle of wills with his master.

The store manager retreated, whisking the curtains closed.

Callista glared at the inoffensive boxes, but curiosity won. Her thoughts were no comfort, anyway. She slipped out of bed and shoved back the first lid. Rainbow-hued dresses of silks, taffetas, soft woolens, and rich brocades spilled over her lap with a life of their own.

She gingerly held one against her and raced to the mirror set into the armoire door. She drew a relieved breath. At least the bodices were cut no lower than the norm, which was to say they were just shy of scandalous. The brilliant green taffeta was two shades darker than her eyes and one of her best colors. How had he known?

The next box held hats, gloves, shoes, and petticoats of every type, from plain to elaborately embroidered, so they would accent the vee-skirted polonaise gowns currently the rage. The last box held a glittering gold ball gown of such fine silk that it would cling to every curve of her body.

The panniers still worn for formal occasions were no more than a sop to convention. And the bodice, well . . . She set the dress aside, wondering where he expected her to wear a gown fit for a harlot. Under the ball gown she found something even more scandalous: lace-trimmed chemises and silk stockings so fine they were transparent. And a night robe of see-through lace, with an accompanying wrap of lace-trimmed gauze.

The Gentle Beast

Callista held both up to her figure before the mirror. Her skin showed through clearly. She gasped and stuffed them into the bottom of the box. Never would she wear something so scandalous. These garments were meant to be taken off, not worn! Why, she'd catch her death of cold parading about in such.

Grimly Callista pulled out the most conservative of the dresses, a dove gray wool housedress that sported a fall of lace at bosom and cuffs. She tried it on. To her dismay, it fit perfectly.

Damn the impudent fellow. Had he taken her measurements in her sleep? Probably not. He was such a rake he could size a woman up with one glance. Not quite sure why the thought made her so angry, she grabbed a handkerchief and tucked it inside the modest bodice. She nodded, satisfied that only her neck showed, and tied on a lace bonnet meant to be worn under one of the wide straw hats.

She stepped back and appraised herself. As a final touch, she laced up a pair of walking boots. Now he'd not so much as glimpse an ankle. Smiling for the first time since her arrival, she sashayed downstairs, not realizing that the plain muslin petticoat she'd selected clung, allowing the soft wool to do likewise.

He was sitting before an exquisite writing desk of walnut inlaid with ebony and tortoiseshell, looking all the more imposing before the spindly legged thing. He was writing in a ledger. As soon as he saw her, he shoved it into a drawer and locked it up.

He leaned back in the velvet chair, which creaked under his bulk. He looked her up and down, his lips twitching under the mask. "I've an antique set of knitting needles somewhere if you want them to match, my little hausfrau."

She curtsied. "And in that role, I shall be glad to tally

up that ledger you were laboring over."

The taunting smile faded. "We've not quite achieved that degree of bliss. Yet."

"You mean you don't trust me."

"Should I?"

"No. No more than I should trust the man who covets all I hold dear."

He waved an impatient hand in the air. "Enough sparring. Can we not declare a truce and make this place a playground rather than a battleground?" He held out a large hand.

Almost, she took it. The choice he gave her was plain: revel or rebel. Ruthlessly Callista squashed the craven urge to back down, to appeal to the softer side of him. If she ceded now, she lost the battle with a more problematic opponent than the Dragon.

Herself.

She turned away to warm her hands at the fire, ignoring his hand. Her skin crawled with the heat of a suppressed anger so intense that her back burned hotter than her fire-warmed front. She heard him take one step toward her. He bit off a curse, then stomped over to the hidden stairway.

She whirled, but couldn't see over his shoulder to discover which hidden panel he pressed. The opening clicked shut, leaving her alone with the regrets of her own choosing.

Henry stepped out of the way of a workman, hoping all this preparation wouldn't be for naught. The dustcovers had been removed. An army of cleaning women waxed every piece of furniture, cleaned every cobweb and speck of dust. Workers painted, papered, and polished brass.

When Callista came back they'd be ready. Henry

The Gentle Beast

paced up and down, awaiting Quartermain, crushing the wayward thought—*if she came back*. Whatever his reasons, Quartermain had ordered his minions to tear London apart looking for Callista. Henry suspected they were more likely to find her than the legitimate authorities, but damn, this waiting was hard.

"Father, what do you think of moving this painting downstairs?" Simon held up the portrait of a ghost from Henry's past. "Rather imposing-looking fellow. Might dress up a card room, what?"

Henry blanched and turned away. "Take it back to the attic and leave it there. Is that clear?"

Bewildered, Simon struggled back up the stairs with the heavy portrait.

Henry stood in the foyer, immune to the babble and banging. His hand went for his cherished stickpin, but fell to his side. A sick feeling had come over him of late. It was more than dread of the Dragon. It was a premonition that an ill deed performed many years ago had finally caught up with him.

If the Dragon were whom he suspected, then nothing would save him. Henry had sold the Yellow Rose, partly hoping to recoup their losses, but mainly to be rid of the tangible proof of his deed. Funny thing was, he'd seldom given the past much thought since Callista lit up his later years.

Until he was forced to.

Henry shivered, wondering if Callista would pay the price for his foolishness. *Dear God, no. Let him take me instead—*

"What are you brooding about, old man?"

Anguish plain on his gaunt but still handsome face, Henry whirled on his uncertain ally. "What the hell do you think? Are your lackeys totally incompetent?"

"Don't you dare speak to me like that. Ever again."

Colleen Shannon

The tone was mild, but the meaning was not. Quartermain's saturnine eyebrows had given his handsome face an evil cast Henry had never noticed before.

"Be . . ." *damned to you*, Henry longed to say, but this man held their future in his hands. He'd learned in a hard school the penalty for rashness; for his children's sake, Henry choked on his frustration. "Be grateful if you'd tell me what they've discovered thus far."

Quartermain relaxed. Henry did not. The more he saw of this man, the less he liked him.

"They tracked down a sedan chairman who, with a little . . . persuasion, shall we say, admitted he took a lady matching Callista's description to the warehouse of a certain Herrick Importers, Limited late last night."

Henry's stomach lurched. Foreboding fulfilled was not a palatable breakfast. "He's certain?"

"Are not you? You're the one who warned me about Herrick's interest in Callista."

"But where could he be hiding her? We searched his premises ourselves."

"He's doubtless spirited her out of London. I shall put my men on finding out where his country estate is. I admit to a certain concern for the girl myself. We cannot start the hell without her."

And this was the man he'd encouraged his daughter to wed? Henry turned away to hide his disgust. "We must go to the magistrate."

"Not yet. Do you really think they shall take the word of a sedan chairman over one of the richest men in England?"

"Perhaps not. But they shall take mine."

"Ah, but rumors are circulating about the mysterious Dragon's interest in your family. First he foreclosed on Callista's estate, then he bought her racehorse, and now I'm told he purchased your diamond."

The Gentle Beast

Henry paled. He'd sold the Yellow Rose to a prominent jeweler who'd promised to be discreet. How had Herrick purchased it so quickly? Still turned away, Henry shrugged, affecting fascination with a set of fireplace irons that, ironically enough, bore dragon heads for handles. "So?"

"So, my dear Henry, one cannot help wondering about this man's particular interest in ruining you, can one? And, since we have a business interest in common, my curiosity is rather greater than most, particularly when I remember all the times that cursed fellow has bested me at cards. Would you care to tell me why Herrick hates you?"

Henry reached out a trembling hand, picked up a poker, and stirred the dying coals to life. "If I knew, I should tell you." Should maybe, but wouldn't. Not even Callista could know his suspicions. Not yet, anyway.

"Never mind, old fellow. I've a way of learning the secrets of others. Now, about that sum you owe me . . ."

But Henry wasn't listening. As the coals shattered and fire licked up the pieces of charred wood, Henry wondered which was worse.

The devil he knew or the one he didn't.

"The devil you say!" Drake stared at Clyde. "What interest does that impudent cit have in . . . of course. Sure as sunrise, Quartermain wants Callista for himself, which is probably why he is trying to get Stanton so indebted to him. Damn. This is an eventuality I had not foreseen."

"Do you want me to bribe the sedan chairman so he'll say he's mistaken?"

"No. 'Tis too late for that. She is safe enough for now, given the fact that Stanton searched for her himself.

But I had best make myself seen this eve, as though no luscious wench awaits my pleasure."

Clyde frowned. "Loose morals or no, Miss Raleigh is a lady, and you should not speak of her that way."

"Ladies are born of spirit, not birth. I have seen women of the lowest caste in India who were far more ladylike than some of these duchesses and baronesses who are trollops at heart."

"Despite her reputation, I believe Miss Raleigh is, at heart, a very great lady. She's given you a merry chase, has she not?"

Drake rose, a cynical cast to his mouth. "Ah, but that says nothing of her morals. I never said she wasn't as high-spirited and exciting as her horse. Believe me, old friend, if you had kissed her, as I have, you would wonder how much she really loved that old beau she professes to yearn for. She sets my blood to singing as no *lady* ever has."

"Perhaps that's your heart speaking rather than your, er, blood. And if her heart speaks likewise, then of course she responds to you. You should be glad of it rather than condemn her for it."

A muscle twitched under the mask as Drake languidly waved his manager away. "I have no heart. Not anymore, thank God. Now please see to your duties. I do not want to be disturbed. If Quartermain sends another minion, notify me immediately."

Sighing, the old man rose and exited, closing the door quietly behind him. Drake tried to concentrate on the coded note from Wilkes, but finally he shoved it aside.

If his heart were dead, why did it leap in his breast every time Callista smiled at him? And where had that forbidden word come from when he'd tried to make her see that her prison could be a home if she loved him?

Drake Herrick, alias the Dragon, late prisoner, pirate, and merchant, stared at the letter that could knot a noose about his neck. Instead he saw a beautiful, willful face that tried to defy him, but betrayed itself with yearning eyes. Those spring green depths that always made him think of new life, called to every urge he'd foresworn.

Hadn't twenty years of peril taught him to trust no one but himself?

After all, that was why he had her—she couldn't be trusted to keep silent. No, these strange feelings she stirred in him must be resisted. With the iron will that had saved his life more times than he cared to count, Drake pulled the letter back up, held it close to a lantern, and began the laborious task of deciphering it.

But always, she sat waiting in the back of his mind, like a sprite enticing him to gambol in the woods.

Or a Yellow Rose men had died for . . .

Fabulous boredom was still boredom.

Callista glared at the treasures scattered carelessly about and wondered where she stood on Drake's inventory. Probably somewhere above the furniture but beneath the art work.

If she had anything to say to it, she'd soon rank beneath the floorboards. As Henry was so fond of telling her, she could be a sore trial when she chose.

Drake would soon regret holding her, she vowed. Callista considered desecrating one of his coveted treasures, but she couldn't bring herself to do it. She was rather fond of beautiful things herself.

The feel of Drake's lips upon hers, his firm body under her seeking hands, flashed through her mind, but there was no one to see her blush. Appalled at her own weakness, she marched back to the fancy writing desk and looked about for something to pry it open. Since he'd taken the key, she couldn't get back into the printing press room, which she'd dearly love to do, but maybe the desk would disclose something equally damaging.

Snatching an ornate dagger from a bracket on the wall, Callista used it to pry open the locked drawer. She rustled the papers inside, disappointed to find the enticing ledger gone. Boring receipts, stationery, and . . . She grabbed a heavy vellum envelope, blank, with no embossed seal, but still waxed closed. She searched the drawer, but the only wax inside was a different shade. If she opened it, he would know.

So? Wasn't that what she wanted? To be so much trouble that he would let her go?

Taking a deep breath, she slit the wax open neatly with the dagger. She pulled the heavy paper out, opened it, and . . .

. . . stared. The paper was blank.

Now why would anyone seal such expensive vellum, fold it, and leave it blank? She was about to put it back when the light caught it. Silvery streaks were briefly illuminated, then gone when she turned it another way. She was so intent on the mystery that she didn't even notice Drake until his large hands took the paper from her.

She almost jumped out of her shoes. She stifled the urge to back away when she looked up at him, but, as usual, she could read his emotions only from his body language. That cursed mask shielded more than his face.

His voice was calm. "Here, my curious cat, let me show you how it works."

The Gentle Beast

He turned up a lantern and held the paper above it, just high enough to keep it from catching fire. He moved the paper from side to side, heating it equally. Two minutes passed. Then writing began to appear, faint streaks at first, finally bold letters that were slightly misshapen but still legible.

Ingenious. Callista had never heard of invisible ink, but then, this man always managed to surprise her.

He held the letter in front of her astonished eyes. It read: *Friday night. Midnight. Usual place.*

There was no signature, but she didn't need one. "Wilkes, isn't it?"

"Your intelligence never fails to delight me." He held the letter to the lantern until it caught fire, and then tossed it into the cold fireplace. "Would you care to hear about the ink?"

Callista turned away, abruptly wishing the fire was lit, for she was chilled to the bone as the implications of his actions sank in. "Some sorcery you filched in your travels, no doubt."

"Not exactly. Actually I studied with an alchemist in Italy some years back, before I decided to return to England. He had no luck turning lead to gold, but when we accidentally devised this mixture and spilled it near the fire, we realized it had other uses."

"For those with secrets."

"Indeed. Would you like some?"

This time she couldn't let the insinuation pass. She whirled on him. "I've discovered few of your secrets you have not deliberately thrust upon me, including this one. You left that letter for me to find, did you not?"

"I knew boredom would get the best of you."

'Twas not boredom. She stared at him. From the time he had set foot in England, this man had made it his

123

Colleen Shannon

mission to get the best of her family. This latest find of hers was only one more link in the chain he helped her weave, binding her to him more closely by the hour. But . . .

"Why? Damn you, why do you hate us so?"

That detestable smirk faded. "You feel yourself ill used by the gifts showered upon you?"

"Trifles. Part of your grand plan to make me so indebted to you that I gladly choose you over Henry." Callista stepped up to him bravely, not for the first time feeling she had to beard the Dragon in his den without so much as a sword to protect herself. She stabbed him in the chest with a fingertip. "You, sir"—she emphasized each word with a tap—"will never, ever, make me forget what I owe to Henry. . . ." She trailed off when he caught her hand and brought it to his mouth.

He whispered into it, "One more thing among many we have in common. I owe all I have and all I am to Henry Stanton." He kissed the palm. "There is a bond between us, Callista, that goes back farther than you can dream. This time we spend together will cement it until you claim your rightful place at my side."

"Nothing you say will ever convince me I am more than a tool in your war against Henry unless you cease your hostilities."

"Do I seem hostile now?" He straightened, his smile hinting of the charming man beneath the mask. He held her hand gently between his own.

She jerked it away lest it betray her. "Yes. Nothing is more devastating in war than treachery disguised as peace."

His smile faded. He reached out and picked up the dagger she'd discarded on the desk, toying with it. "You won't let me be kind to you, will you?"

"I hate you." Desperately she wished it were so. She

wouldn't feel torn in twain then. She braced herself for his reaction.

As usual he didn't react as expected. He breached the short distance between them in two bold steps and lifted her hand. He slapped the dagger hilt firmly in her palm. "Prove it."

The cold truth of the jeweled dagger made it impossible for her to deny reality. This was what their relationship had come to. She stared down dumbly at the exquisite thing. The solid gold hilt was encrusted with rubies, but the stiletto blade was Toledo steel and would do the task it had been designed for.

Beautiful but deadly. An apt description of their relationship.

"Here, let me make it easier for you to kill this beast who holds you." He fumbled with his waistcoat and shirt until his chest, strong and furred with soft hair, was partially exposed. Then he took her limp hand, closed it about the dagger hilt, and brought the razor-sharp tip to bear against his skin. "Do it. Thrust it to the hilt, so we both shall learn if I still have a bleeding heart or a singed lump of coal. I confess I do not know myself."

Every soft word slashed her like the dagger, but one thing she knew: she could never harm him. Even if he deserved it. She struggled to pull away, but her strength was puny compared to his. To her horror, he forced her hand closer until she saw a red dot appear on the tip of the blade.

"No!" she cried.

"Yes," he whispered. "As God is my witness, 'tis the only way I'll ever let you go."

When she still resisted, he changed tactics so quickly that she wasn't prepared for the prick at her palm. She stared as blood dotted the tiny cut. Her head spun when he lifted her palm against his chest and rubbed it around in his blood. He pulled her hand away and held it up before her eyes. She saw his blood, and her own, smeared on her palm and his chest.

Her throat tightened with an emotion she couldn't, or wouldn't, name. Still, she could not block out the words that breached one more of her crumbling defenses.

"I'm told the savages of America mix their blood to show a mystic, primal bond." He soothed her cut with his mouth, smiling against her palm as she gasped. "Now we are one. Beauty chained to beast, blood shared, bound forever. An evocative beginning for the future sharing of our blood in that most intimate of ways . . ."

He trailed off with such wicked promise that she had to whisper, "How?"

"Why, when we make a child together. And what a strong lad he will be. Would you like to begin now?"

Panic assailed her. Not at his words, but at her own response to them. Every nerve in her body was alive with the feel and smell of him. An image of a black-haired young boy with green eyes popped into her head, but another bonding would be required first. A liquid warmth in the intimate center of her body was almost her undoing. She longed to take him in her arms and soothe their mutual pain with a passion as forbidden as it was heady.

But that damnable Raleigh pride made her struggle to pull away. Typical, that he should demand a boy rather than a girl. "And what if we should have a girl instead?"

"Why, I shall treat her like the princess she will be." His palm lowered to her belly. "And devote myself nightly to my lady's pleasure."

The Gentle Beast

She shoved that intimately caressing hand away. "I shall not birth any bastards." She tried to pull away, but he would not allow it. He caught one restive hand in his own and drew it behind his back, wrapping his other arm about her waist.

"We shall see. Kiss me to seal our bond." His head lowered until she felt the heat of his tempting mouth.

"A bond with a beast! Well, devil take you, I say."

"A journey we shall both enjoy, I vow. 'Tis time your bold words are put to the test. If you resist me, I shall let you go."

A barrage she could have repelled; a gentle foray she could not.

Warm, mobile lips just brushed her own. When she turned her head, he allowed it, only to trail his mouth down the pure curve of her cheek, investigating the side of her neck all the way down to the handkerchief at her bodice, which stopped his progress. She tensed, waiting for him to rip the white square away, but he only subjected the opposite side of her neck to a like torment.

For such a large, powerful man, he could be so gentle. . . . Her last coherent thought fled with the second touch of his mouth on hers. Her lips tingled under the soft persuasion, and unconsciously she pressed for deeper contact. His soft laugh swirled about them, a protective cocoon over their building passion. He subverted her hungry, seeking mouth by kissing and delicately nibbling her ear.

Delectable shivers replaced the last of her reserve. The third time he sought her mouth, she was ripe for his picking. Gladly she fell into his hands, trusting him on a level deeper than pride, thought, or reason. This time he hauled her so close that only her toes touched the floor, and he took all she wanted to give.

127

It still wasn't enough. When she shoved urgent hands into his gaping shirt, testing the sheer power of him, he gasped into her mouth. She felt a strange hardness at her hips bumping her gently, inciting a rich moistness in the forbidden center of her body.

She would have fallen then had he not picked her up and carried her to the settee, covering her with his welcome weight. All the while his lips ravaged hers, sampling the passion that was, finally, full-blown.

The handkerchief went cockeyed along with her world. Lips that should have been hard but weren't, and hands that should have been rough but weren't, bared her feelings and her modesty. The coldness at her breast as her clothes were opened was soon replaced by the fire of his mouth hoarding her treasures.

He kissed one roseate crest, then blessed the other. His large hand gently cupped and fondled the opposite breast, making of her nipples homing beacons awaiting his return. His groan of pleasure at the taste of her matched and mingled with her own.

Her senses were too drugged to comprehend what it meant to be alone on a settee with an aroused man kissing her breasts. She knew only that she could not get close enough to him, that the throbbing in her loins foretold an end she had to find. . . .

He covered her completely then, rubbing his hairy chest over her exquisitely sensitive breasts, and for the first time she knew the heady touch of skin on skin. "Drake," she whispered, hungry for his mouth again. She pulled the cord off his queue and his hair tumbled free into her hands, as dark and vital as his spirit.

He caught his breath, then cupped her face in his hands and made her look at him. "Say it again. Who am I?"

That dragon mask no longer frightened her. Behind

The Gentle Beast

it lurked a man inherently gentle, as only a strong man can be. This man behind the mask drew her as no man ever had, even her beloved Heath. "Drake," she whispered shyly, trying to pull that drugging mouth down to hers again.

His held breath eased into a heartfelt sigh that pressed his flesh into hers one last time. Then his warmth was gone. She felt his hands pulling up her chemise and buttoning her dress.

Modesty reclaimed was far more devastating than modesty lost. The sight of his hands on her bodice acted like a cold dash of water. She shoved him away and turned her shamed face into the soft cushion.

"Go away. Go away and never come back."

His weight lifted off the settee, but she felt him hovering over her.

"I shall finish what we began if you wish it," he said lightly, as if he offered to sample her cooking. But those large hands clenched at his sides, as if he had to force himself not to touch her.

She tensed at the cruelty, every sensitized nerve quivering. "Leave me be. You've taken enough from me."

"As you wish." His footsteps receded. She heard the panel open and close, then blessed silence.

Except it felt cursed. She lay there, her fears all the greater because some deep, integral part of her regretted only one thing—that he hadn't finished what he began. . . .

Drake's arousal was slow to soften. Didn't the silly chit understand what it cost him to let her go? Honor was not totally dead in him, he decided bitterly. She was the daughter of his greatest enemy, a wanton by reputation and reaction to his caresses, but still, some-

Colleen Shannon

thing had made him pull away. Hearing his name rather than her old lover's on her mouth had been like a balm to his wounded pride.

Her feelings mattered not a whit to him, he told himself. Honor had nothing to do with it. Instinctively he knew she was not ready. If he'd taken her then, he'd never get what he wanted from her.

Total, unmitigated devotion. She would stand by his side and curse her stepfather to hell ere he was done.

Only then would his victory over Henry Stanton, Earl of Swanlea, murderer of his father and of his childhood, be complete.

Yet as Drake poured antiseptic over his self-inflicted wound, the bite of pain brought a savage grin to his face. *You fool. You deserve this, for such a confounded trick.* What had possessed him to utter such gibberish?

A mystical, primal bond indeed. All he wanted of Callista Raleigh was a toss, a tumble, and a dishonoring. Still, as he tied his cravat, cursing his clumsy hands, he was abruptly glad that he had to be about town this eve. Each time he held Callista in his arms, revenge seemed a bit less sweet. . . .

Callista shoved the peas and carrots around her plate, making a battery that guarded her parsleyed potatoes. Then she made a mound of her roast beef, a parapet from whence came her archers of pointy green beans.

"Are you going to eat that or study it for weakness?" Clyde Haynes, apparently the only man the Dragon trusted, set a basket of hot rolls down next to her and opened the linen covering to let the yeast fragrance waft over her.

Callista didn't look up from her miniature battleground. "Give me a dragon-shaped pudding and I shall consume it quite happily."

The faithful manager hesitated. Then, to Callista's surprise, he plopped down with her at the tiny table he'd set with the finest linen and china. He calmly buttered a roll for himself. "How much do you know about . . . Drake Herrick?"

The hesitation was telling, but Callista had always known the Dragon used an alias. "All I need to know."

"Which is?"

"He's a ruthless privateer who takes what he wants, be damned to right or wrong."

"Or the consequences to himself." Clyde took a contemplative bite of roll. "You are partly right, but you have twisted the why of it. He acts, always, according to his own sense of right and wrong. As his father did."

Bitterly Callista shoved back her plate, unable to eat a bite. "I've done naught to him."

"You, perhaps not. But your stepfather . . ." He polished off the roll, as if he'd said enough.

Callista played with her napkin, pretending indifference. "I am confoundedly tired of these veiled references to Henry's youthful indiscretions. Either tell me what happened or hush."

Apparently he decided to take the latter advice. He wiped his hands and mouth with another napkin and made to rise.

Callista caught his arm. "Please don't go. Tell me how you came to serve him. If I understood him better, perhaps I could accept my captivity." *In a pig's eye.* But she must use some of the Dragon's tactics if she were to escape.

He sat back down. His gaunt face caught the shadows, and for the first time she noticed how thin he was, how straggly was his pulled-back gray hair. "I owe my life to Drake. I will end it serving him." His long face was melancholy, and he coughed into the napkin.

Such loyalty was rare in this day and age, Callista reflected. Now that she knew Drake better, however, she wasn't surprised that he inspired it. "How did he save you?"

Clyde stared at her for a long time, as if wondering whether he could trust her with the truth. "We were both . . . imprisoned. I was about to die, and when Drake escaped, he took me with him. He had to literally carry me through part of the journey. Please promise me you shall tell no one of this. He would not thank me for my loose tongue."

Callista nodded, touched. So Drake Herrick was capable of compassion—long ago, in another life. But he tried to present himself as a ruthless man who cared only for himself and his own ambitions.

Which was the real man? Callista knew what she wanted to believe, but the two images were at such odds that she was stymied. She sipped her wine, reflecting on one reality that nothing could explain away.

She had been ripe for the taking just a few hours past, and he had left her.

Had he acted out of chivalry or still greater deceit?

When Drake approached the King's Head in Ivy Lane, St. Paul peered over the shops and hostelries, as if even the monuments themselves were curious about this strange newcomer. He paused to straighten his perfect cravat, shook his lace cuffs over his hands, and propped his cane under his arm.

Then, muttering to himself, "Devil take the hindmost," Drake entered the cheerful common room. The crackling fire punctuated the even more combustible conversation. Drake paused in the shadowy doorway, watching London's intellectuals arguing.

In one corner, Sir Joshua Reynolds said with great disdain, "Rubens? Bah! He's nothing but a peasant with a predilection for fat women." The two young men beside him both had paint stains on their hands, so it wasn't hard to deduce why they hung on his every word.

At another table, Sir John Hawkins, the well-known biographer, nodded at something Oliver Goldsmith said. Drake caught the name "David Garrick."

The portly gentleman with the distinctive shaking was a man Drake had seen at card parties a couple of times and much admired. Drake eased closer to catch the gist of the conversation. The redoubtable Dr. Samuel Johnson's blue eyes snapped along with his wit. "He'll be one of our club, eh? How does he know we will permit him?"

"Come, come, dear friend," Goldsmith said. "Does the fact that he treads the boards make him ill suited for our club?"

"I am a great friend to public amusements, as you well know, Oliver. They keep people from vice. 'Tis not his mind I question. 'Tis his presumption."

The cue couldn't have been better. Drake stepped forward boldly. Men looked his way over tankards and hearty fare. Some stopped midsentence, elbowing their companions; others merely stared. But Drake could safely say that his presence had been duly noted by some of the biggest gossips the realm had ever seen.

He stopped at the vacant chair at Johnson's table. "Dr. Johnson, how felicitous. How are you this fine eve?"

Johnson wiped his mouth and nodded calmly. "Passable, sir. At least I have not taken to hiding my face yet."

Drake didn't blink, and Johnson smiled in wry admiration. His acerbic wit had made dukes, earls, and even, on occasion, the king himself, squirm.

Goldsmith was not so cordial. He rammed the chair into the table. Drake pretended obtuseness. Not that he could blame the man, considering the amount of money the writer had lost at their last game. Drake nodded slightly in his direction and made to seek a lone table in a dark corner. But he didn't miss the harsh look Johnson cast at his friend.

Johnson shoved the chair back out. "I look upon every day in which I do not make a new acquaintance as a day lost. Come, sir, join us and let us renew ours."

Drake pretended hesitation. "I do not wish to intrude."

"Nonsense! Come along."

Drake sat down, hooking his cane on the back of the chair. "You are kind, sir. I confess I have longed to ask your opinion of Richardson."

"Richardson? I see we have another taste in common aside from appreciation of the fairer sex." When Drake didn't react to his droll look, Johnson continued, "Why, sir, if you were to read Richardson for the story, your impatience would be so much fretted that you would hang yourself. But you must read him for the sentiment. There is more knowledge of the heart in one letter of Richardson's than in all *Tom Jones*."

Drake nodded gravely, but it was the allusion to women that held his attention more than the opinion, as much as he agreed with it. What the deuce was Johnson referring to? Some instinct made Drake change the subject.

"What do you recommend for the best meal here?"

A spirited discussion followed over the merits of chicken, veal, and beef. Drake sat back and listened, taking the measure of each man. Finally he took Goldsmith's suggestion, hoping to mollify the poor loser somewhat.

When Drake shoved back his empty plate some time later, he decided he'd traveled too far and wide ever to renew his taste for Yorkshire pudding. However, he pretended satisfaction, wondering when he could politely take his leave.

Johnson smiled. "There is nothing that has yet been contrived by man by which so much happiness is produced as by a good tavern or inn."

Sir John Hawkins said, "I can think of a little ballet dancer I saw the other day—"

"Ah, but she's a creation of God, dear fellow."

"But—Blast, what's that cit doing here?"

Drake followed his gaze to the doorway. For once he was glad of the mask. What ill fortune had brought Quartermain and Stanton here on his rare night about town? Drake considered dashing out the back, but that would be too suspicious.

Not to mention craven. He had naught to feel guilty for, he told himself. No one knew he held Callista. As Drake fiddled with his cuffs, pretending boredom, his gaze collided with Johnson's. Something in that assessing blue gaze made him uneasy.

Henry Stanton stopped square in front of him. "You are a bold bastard, I grant you that. How dare you sup with some of the most respected men in England as if you had no care in the world!"

"I had none—until now. You really are becoming a bore on this subject, my dear Henry." How had they known he was here?

"Do not call me that," Henry gritted through his teeth. "I—"

Colleen Shannon

But Quartermain cut in. "Do these men know what you really are?"

Here it came. Drake drummed his scarred fingers idly on the table, well aware that everyone looked at them. Let them wonder how he received the wound. Henry glanced at his hand, then quickly away.

"And what is that?" Drake asked.

"A vile kidnapper of innocent young women." Quartermain leaned his palms against the table and glared into Drake's masked eyes.

The rattle of fork against plate and tankard against table had long ago stopped, but it was Johnson's reaction that bothered Drake. He gasped and leaned back in his chair.

Drake replied evenly, "I thought we were done with that foolishness. You have searched my properties and found no trace of her, is that not correct? Perhaps the chit ran away with a swain—"

Drake's head rocked sideways from the impact of Stanton's slap. Drake caught the dragon mask just in time, reattached it, and towered to his feet.

Stanton's face was ashen, but he stood his ground and said with quiet resolution, "You will rue the day you ever persecuted me and mine. I vow it before every man in this room." He whirled and stomped out.

Quartermain straightened to his full, imposing height, his eyes on a level with Drake's. "Do you not wish to know how I discovered your whereabouts this eve?"

"No. You have a multitude of spies to do your bidding. I am not exactly a figure who blends in well with high society."

Laughter roared at this, but Quartermain glared at each man in turn until they were silent. "I shall be watching you, whether you take a piss or eat a joint."

136

The Gentle Beast

"Behold me quivering in my boots," Drake retorted. "When you find Miss Raleigh, you are welcome to her. I've no taste for flighty women." How well I lie, Drake reflected. But then he'd learned to do so in the hardest school of all—survival.

Quartermain marched to the door, but Drake wasn't surprised when he had to have the last word. "For your own sake, you'd best be telling the truth. Callista Raleigh is mine. I'll kill any man who tries to take her from me."

The door slammed behind him. A startled silence held for a moment, then broke into pandemonium.

Drake sat back down. "Please accept my apologies, gentlemen. I would not have subjected you to my petty squabbles for all the world."

Johnson mouthed the word *petty*.

For once, it was Sir John Hawkins who was astute enough to describe the general feeling of those sitting at the table. "Damned impudence. The stench of the shopkeeper reeks from Quartermain and his ilk. Can't understand why Stanton socializes with him."

As much as he disliked Quartermain, Drake couldn't let the snobbery pass. "Some among us have to work for a living."

Sir John opened his mouth to retort, but Dr. Johnson cut him off by rising. "Indeed. Without it, where would England be? As for where I need to be, gentlemen, my bed calls. With every year it grows more appealing, and nobody who doesn't rise early will ever do any good." But he winked, and there was general laughter at this, as it was well known among the group that the good doctor usually slept until noon.

Having succeeded in lightening the heavy ambience, Johnson gathered his hat and walking stick, and then looked at Drake. "Would you care to walk with me, young man?"

Drake rose with alacrity, well aware of the honor. "I should be delighted, sir."

Johnson led the way out. Again the conversation dribbled off as envious eyes watched them leave. Sir John Hawkins's voice carried, as if by chance: "He'd be safer with footpads than with that scoundrel."

Drake's step faltered, but he didn't give the man the satisfaction of looking back. Johnson did, however, and Hawkins said no more.

Johnson closed the door behind them with a bang. "Sir John is a very unclubbable man. But one cannot always choose one's tavern companions." He sent Drake a droll look. "Would you not agree?"

Drake didn't answer. However, Johnson's next words made him stop stone-cold and look about to see if anyone heard.

"Having seen for myself how charming the Lady Callista is, I understand your interest in her, but since she has not been seen since the night she went to your shop, I am honor-bound to demand an audience with her. If you hold her against her will, sirrah, I have no choice but to approach the authorities."

Johnson's blue eyes were no longer friendly.

Chapter Six

Drake blustered, "By my troth, sir, I do not know what you mean."

"You lie very well, young man. But not well enough. I gave you the honor of not accusing you in front of the others because, damned if I know why, I like you. Somewhere behind that cursed mask lurks an honorable man, but when an innocent young woman's safety is at stake, my feelings matter naught. Take me to Lady Callista immediately or it shall be a very long time before I find my bed this night."

The threat was veiled but explicit. Drake opened his mouth, shut it, and without a word stomped in the opposite direction. He felt the noose tightening with every step. He squelched the instinct to flee. He'd spent twenty years learning to survive for one purpose: to return to England and retake what was stolen from him.

No, by God, if he had to finish his vengeance from

Newgate, finish it he would. As he rounded the corner to his warehouse, Dr. Johnson tired but inexorable at his side, Drake tried to squash the tiny hope that sprang from a source he didn't dare plumb.

There was no chance in hell that Callista Raleigh would pretend she was there of her own accord. . . .

"Damnation, where is he?" Callista grumbled, turning over in the too comfortable bed yet again. He was probably in some harlot's bed, sharing that wonderfully controlled power with a woman who knew how to utilize it. Callista punched her pillow but it didn't help.

Finally, defeated, she tossed back the silk covers and stuck her feet into the frilly slippers he'd purchased for her. She tried on the ridiculous night robe that was nothing but a fall of lace, took it off, and put on his heavy Chinese dressing gown instead.

She inhaled the scent of his mints and cologne. If she'd seen the smile that broke out on her face, she would have slapped herself, but her heart was inexplicably lighter as she went downstairs. The sideboard held nothing so ladylike as ratafia, so she poured herself a hefty draft of brandy. She was warming it in her hands when the panel clicked open. She whirled, her heart beating a welcome, but it was only Clyde.

A very agitated Clyde. "Milady, come with me. You've a visitor."

"Henry?" Callista waited for a joy that did not come. After all, if someone knew she was here, she'd certainly be free very soon. She gathered up her brandy to take it with her. Something told her she was going to need it.

"Nay. Come. We must make haste."

Callista frowned, wondering if she should go so attired, but she shrugged. He wanted her for a mistress, so she might as well play the part.

Every taper in the place was ablaze when she exited the narrow stairway. Clyde led her down the hall to his own office, which was brighter yet. She was still adjusting to the light when a voice she'd heard only once before said, "Good evening, my dear. I'm glad to see you looking well."

Callista blinked. Dr. Samuel Johnson's kind, plump face, nodding continuously in that palsied way, came into focus. Behind it lurked a beastly visage that had once figured in her nightmares, but lately had been the center of more erotic dreams. Quickly she looked back at Johnson.

"Good even, sir. May I ask what brings you here so late?"

"Why, concern for you, child. Your stepfather and his business associate came to the King's Head tonight, and they seemed to believe this young rake here had something to do with your disappearance. Given our chance meeting at this very place the other night, I had to lend the accusation a bit more credence than I might have otherwise."

Nonplussed, Callista sank down in a chair. Johnson sat gratefully opposite her, but Drake remained standing behind the desk chair. Clyde guarded the door, his big-nosed face reminding Callista of Cerberus at his most protective.

In truth, she'd had other things on her mind than her chance meeting with the world's most renowned lexicographer. Forbidden things. She dipped her flushed face and took a sip of brandy, trying to collect her scattered thoughts. Why was she hesitating? Tell Johnson this rake had kidnapped her, and she was free.

It was as simple as that.

141

Except nothing between them had ever been simple. Callista sneaked another glance at Drake, then looked as quickly away.

For his part, Johnson appraised her carefully, from the tousled, loose hair and the too big dressing gown that obviously belonged to her "kidnapper," to the primly held feet. But her hands twisted and turned the brandy snifter, and she gazed into it as if hoping for divine inspiration. Neither her tension nor her sensitivity to Drake's every move escaped the doctor's acute gaze.

Even more telling was her continued silence. Johnson relaxed in his chair, a smile chasing away the severity of his expression. "It has not been my experience that a woman wears the garment of a man she hates."

Callista looked down, seeing herself as she must look to him. Her skin acquired a rosy hue that only made her look even less abused. She glanced yet again at Drake, trying to pretend a dislike she no longer felt. It was hopeless.

She sensed his tension more than saw it, only because she knew his mannerisms by now. He seemed disinterested, but she noted that his big hands clutched the chair back so tightly that his knuckles gleamed white.

Here, she realized vaguely, was her chance. She'd been his helpless toy from that first confrontation in Henry's bedchamber; now he was hers to do with as she would.

If she told the truth, he'd be in gaol by morn. She opened her mouth, shut it. The words would not come.

All three men looked at her, waiting. Even the candle flames stopped dancing, leaning ever so slightly her way as if to listen.

"Well, my dear? If you're here by choice, I'll take my

creaky bones on their way. If not, speak up." Johnson's genial smile had slipped.

Callista was beginning to match him in impatience. Being at a loss for words was not a common failing of hers, to say the least. But these circumstances were far from common. Caught as she was 'twixt Scylla and Charybdis, must she choose the whirlpool or the monster?

The choice was easy, in the end. The fearsome dragon was no monster. She'd stake her life on that—as she might well be doing. "I came here of my own accord and stay because I wish it." Callista waited for her instincts to scream *Craven!*

But she felt only peace. She sipped composedly at her brandy.

Dr. Johnson glanced at Drake. The mask could not hide his gasp or shocked immobility. Clyde leaned weakly against the wall. Dr. Johnson's twinkle was more pronounced than ever as he stood.

"Well, this has been a most interesting eve. Would you escort me to the door, my dear?"

Callista rose. She had to fold back the dressing gown sleeves before she could accept his extended arm. Then, feeling more like a queen than a silly girl wearing her captor's brand, she tripped down the stairs beside him. Amazing. Drake was still speechless, trailing along after them like a lonesome puppy. She liked him this way: quiet and obedient. Pity it wouldn't last.

Discreetly, Clyde disappeared into his office.

At the entrance, Callista stopped and smiled up at her favorite author. "May I say, kind sir, how grateful I am to you for your concern? I would be pleased if you would keep my presence here to yourself. I shall send a note to Henry in the morn to let him know I am well. I should have done so sooner."

Johnson kissed her hand. "Of course, my dear. And I wish you the absolute best in all your . . . endeavors."

As Johnson opened the door, a possessive hand landed on Callista's shoulder. "Don't go," Drake whispered for her ears only.

Callista shrugged him off irritably. Had she not already proved her loyalty?

Johnson glanced at Drake, then back at Callista's willful face. A wistful gleam replaced the twinkle in his eyes. "You have not asked it, but I am a writer, confound it, with an opinion on everything. Both of you mark this little homily, which it has taken me nigh on sixty years to learn: Life admits not of delays; when pleasure can be had, it is fit to catch it. Every hour takes away part of the things that please us, and perhaps part of our disposition to be pleased." With that, he gave them both a dignified nod and went on his way.

Quickly Drake locked the door. He trapped her in the circle of his arms. "In a word, seize the day," he said softly. He leaned close enough for her to feel his body heat. "Good advice from one of the smartest men England has ever produced, is it not, my dear?"

"I like you better when you're tongue-tied."

"Fine. You tie it for me."

She gaped at him, but he explained in a most explicit way—he bent down, slanted his mouth over hers, and coaxed her tongue inside. Then he proceeded to show her how easily they could tie each other into knots.

Callista couldn't help it. She melted into him, sighing into his kiss, certain now on a bone-deep level that she'd done the right thing. The quality of his kiss was different from before. He'd always been gentle, but his skill had been like a drug, enervating her will to subjugate her to the tyranny of pleasure.

This time, this time . . . he was subjugated with her.

The Gentle Beast

His lips, his hands were desperate, as if he, too, knew their time was measured. If they failed to seize pleasure, they had no one to blame but themselves.

She had to give one last token protest. "This is madness," she whispered, wrenching her mouth away.

He trailed his lips down her throat to the throbbing hollow. "Then may they cart us both to Bedlam."

The kiss deepened. His mask went askew, but Callista didn't even feel it. Her world reeled as she was lifted off her feet and borne to the nether regions with the beast she was blessed with. . . .

Henry glanced at the announcement in the *London Daily Courant*, then tossed it back in Quartermain's lap. "A week? We cannot open the hell in a week. We must find Callista."

"I know exactly where she is."

Henry froze. "Where?"

"Herrick has her, of course."

"But we've searched—"

"He has a hidden warehouse, you imbecile. I'm told by one of my most reliable sources that a dray makes monthly midnight pickups behind his shop. I'd lay odds that whatever concourse is going on there is somehow illegal. We've only to watch. And wait. When we prove the very rich Mr. Drake Herrick to be a kidnapper, a thief, or possibly a traitor, even he won't avoid the gallows. He will never insult his betters again."

Quartermain smiled with such pleasure that Henry had to turn away. Yes, he hated Herrick, but he could not contemplate any man's demise with quite such relish.

I must be getting old, Henry thought with a sigh. The challenge that would have invigorated him once upon a time was now a sore trial. The more he saw Herrick, the more certain he became of who the man really was. And if that were the case, he could not blame Herrick for his vendetta.

Dear God, let Quartermain be right. Time was nigh. For either deliverance—or disaster.

Callista, my dear girl, I pray you don't reap what I've sown.

Indeed, the whirlwind had taken possession of all that Callista knew and held dear. Including her own self-control.

When she felt the soft mattress at her back, she relaxed.

When a hard body covered her, she sought closer contact.

And when he lifted her to pull the robe free, she assisted.

The bed curtains whooshed back, clothes rustled, and the soft lantern glow became a blaze.

Callista kept her eyes tight shut, for if she opened them she'd have to face reality again.

Fantasy was so much nicer.

Here in this fantastic bed in this beautiful, hidden place, wrong was right and black was white. The man who'd destroyed her became her greatest protector. He offered redemption, not disaster. The desire he inspired in her was good and right.

Seize the day!

Callista suited action to word and grabbed blindly with both hands. One hand touched a warm, furred chest and buried itself deep. The other touched something alien, something that suited this topsy-turvy world.

How could something so hard be so soft?

The Gentle Beast

A male groan preceded a strong hand gripping her errant one. "Don't touch unless you want to pay the price." He pulled her other arm about his neck and used his own hands to devastating effect. The thin lawn gown inched above her ankles to her calves, and kept rising.

Callista had to joke, or bolt. "Spoken like a true merchant. If I break it, do I have to pay for it?" She gurgled a soft laugh and opened her eyes—to find them filled with acres of broad, bare chest.

My God, he is strong. He could snap her like a twig. Callista blushed and turned her head, unable to look at the most potent proof of the differences between them.

Why did he turn up the lanterns? If he wanted no secrets between them, why didn't he remove that cursed mask? Smiling or no, it still hid the real Drake.

He seemed to sense her broken concentration, for he slanted his mouth over hers again, kissing her as if there were no world beyond the two of them. His mouth made all the promises his words could not, teaching her that in bed there was no victor, no vanquished. Only two people with joy to share.

And she relaxed, feeling cherished and needed, the two most potent feelings any man could inspire in his woman.

All the while, he caressed her leg, thigh to ankle and back, no more, no less. Thus gently encouraged, she skimmed her hands over his shoulders, down his strong back, feeling his muscles rippling, then—

Shoving him away, she sat up abruptly and peered over his back. "Dear God," she whispered. Tentatively she ran her fingers over each hard ridge. This man had been whipped mercilessly. But the scars were hard and

147

buried under the skin, so they must have been made years ago.

"How?" was all she could manage.

His eyes glittered in the light, delving deep into the forest green pools that shimmered with tears for his pain. "It matters not. Under the touch of your hands, they disappear. Please . . ."

He brought her hands back around him. It was the first time he'd asked her for anything. Hesitantly she ran her fingertips lightly over each scar. He made a sound she could only equate with a purr. The touch of her hands could do that to him?

It was she who sought his lips, trying to please him. Her mouth moved tentatively upon his. Her unpracticed ardor seemed to mesmerize him, for he held her now as if she would break—until her tongue ventured shyly into his mouth. With a strangled gasp, he pressed her into the mattress. Those broad shoulders hovered above her, blocking light, reason, and the last of her sanity.

As the kiss deepened, his hand wandered higher, touching the poetic curve of her hip. She squirmed under him, wondering why her skin had a will of its own, alive to every touch of his hand. Her legs parted. This time the sounds came from her when he accepted her invitation and touched where no man had touched.

She arched, gasping into his mouth. He growled his own pleasure and caressed the unfolding bud of her desire. His mouth singed a trail down her neck. The pleasant fire spread until even her hair follicles tingled, but when his fingers pressed deeper she almost came off the bed, unable to bear the sheer beauty of this intimacy she'd never dreamed of.

His touch withdrew abruptly. He sat up, throwing his legs over the side of the bed, his back to her. Callista returned to herself slowly, torn between wonder and frustration. She touched his sweat-sheened shoulder.

"Why did you stop?" She was amazed to feel him trembling.

At first it seemed he wouldn't answer; then he said so softly she had to strain to hear, "I've done many things I've regretted in my life, but as yet, I have never despoiled a virgin."

Callista sat back on her heels. Abruptly she pulled the gown down over her legs, wondering why she should feel hurt. "Did you think I was otherwise?"

He looked askance at her over his shoulder. "From the day we met you have done all you could to make me believe you as bold a piece as I've ever come across. How could any innocent react with such aplomb to the drawings in my office, play piquet so confidently with so much at stake? As for your reputation among the men in the clubs—"

"I care not a farthing for what they think. On the day a young man I loved beyond reason died, I promised myself to live only for what I believe in. If you equate innocence with weakness, sir, then you have much mistaken me."

He caught her hand to keep her from pulling away. He kept his back turned as if her virginity had suddenly made her off-limits. Callista didn't know whether to be insulted or touched at his sudden change, but his next words caused a reaction that was not ambivalent.

"I never would have been drawn to you if you were some milk-and-water miss, as I suspect you well know. But this . . . this I never expected. I cannot undo what has been done, but I can make amends." He turned, pulled the sheet over his lap, and lifted her chin. "My beauty, will you marry me?"

Sheer astonishment overwhelmed her muddled

emotions. "You jest. I have never even seen your face."

"I have never been more sincere in my life. We make quite a pair, I think. The good doctor certainly seems to agree." He looked at her expectantly, his gaze no longer wandering.

Only in the secretness of her own heart would Callista admit her desire to hear these words from this most elusive of men. Yet where were the endearments, the promises of devotion Heath had given her? He offered a business arrangement, nothing more, and once she was no longer useful as a weapon against Henry, he'd doubtless discard her. Angrily she pulled her hands away. "I am less insulted by your honest offer to make me a whore than I am by this . . . sop to your conscience. I will never wed. Certainly not to a man who hates my family. This is just another ruse."

She rose, but he followed, caught her waist, and turned her to face him. She closed her eyes rather than look at him. She could not let him see what his nakedness did to her. But she could not hide the nipples that hardened in response.

"This is no ruse. Look at me, Callista. See what you do to me. We've been discussing one kind of union for the past ten minutes, yet you can plainly see that I long for a more basic kind. My body cares little for your innocence." His voice softened. "But my soul, such as it is, longs to join you in every way a man can."

She wanted to resist, to wrap her wounded dignity about herself like a chastity belt. But that voice, more husky and deeper than she'd ever heard it, struck some elemental, feminine chord until she vibrated with need of him. Damn his black soul, she wanted him.

She opened her eyes.

And she gasped. She'd always known he was big and powerful, but from his strong neck to the soles of his feet, he was man as God intended when he breathed life into dust. He reminded her of Paris, every muscle and sinew toned with vitality. His chest made a wide angle to his narrow waist and narrower hips. Her gaze skittered down his muscular thighs to his taut calves. Even his ankles were strong and straight. From the front his scars could not be seen.

But they were a part of him, as much a part of him as . . . again she could not look.

He laughed, deep and pure. "Zounds, woman, you can touch but not look? 'Tis unfair, me bare and no secrets to hide, you still dressed."

Callista glanced down at the lawn gown, knowing it was no more than a thin veil in the light. Odd that he had not removed her night robe, though she would not have stopped him, which he surely knew.

Callista took a deep breath and did what he, and her own instincts, bade. Her eyes widened. At the apex of his hips stood the proud eminence that made him male. And eminence was certainly the right word. He was so big that she automatically took a step backward in sheer alarm. She'd watched Paris service several mares. She knew the mechanics of the sex act.

The mares had squealed as they were impaled, some trying to get away from the long rod that seemed to have a will of its own. But the stallion had held them firm, forelegs over their hips, and rutted and grunted as he had his way.

Was it so between men and women?

She didn't know, but one thing she was certain of: she'd never be able to hold that hard, proud length in the vulnerable center of her body. Not without pain. Callista turned aside, only to come face-to-face with the mirror in the armoire and the tall figure coming up behind her.

It's passing strange, Callista thought. Even as her mind shied away from the intimacies his maleness sought, her body responded with tingling breasts and throbbing loins. Was she a wanton after all? Or was it normal for her to respond to his obvious excitement? Wed him, she could not, but bed him . . . She was tempted.

He caught her shoulders and pulled her back against him. Her buttocks felt the hardness she'd incited and did not know what to do with it.

"Look, Callista. Our joining, in every way a man and woman can, is ordained by fate. Resist me and you resist yourself. You know it is so, else you would have told the good doctor the truth. Let me get a special license so this night can take its course." Other than that imperative flesh at her hips and his hands light upon her shoulders, he did not touch her.

Truth? She no longer knew the right of it. As certain as she stood there, the honorable anchor of her life, Henry Stanton, had somehow betrayed this man. If she gave in to this heady rapture, Lady Callista Raleigh, owner of Summerlea, would be no more.

Mistress Callista or Mrs. Drake Herrick, it mattered little, for the Callista she knew would be gone.

Still, if he'd taken off his mask and bared the most important part of him, she might have risked it. He did not. She tilted her chin, forcing a determination she did not feel. "How can I wed my family's worst enemy?"

His hands tightened; then he released her abruptly. His comforting warmth at her back was gone, as was the warmth in his voice. "I might say the same."

"You will let bygones be bygones, then, if I wed you?"

He turned away to put on his discarded dressing gown. "Yes—when he is gone."

The Gentle Beast

There it was, then. At least he hadn't lied to her.

Callista bit her lip until the emotional pain was eased by the physical. She crawled back into bed, pulled up the disheveled covers, and turned on her side away from him.

She felt him hovering over her. He took a deep breath, as if to speak; then he whirled. He paused at the catwalk steps. "Write a note to Stanton and I shall see he receives it. You have not heard the last of this, my beauty."

His steps retreated.

Callista lay there, hearing Dr. Johnson's admonishment. He was right, she thought, tears falling hot and fast.

He needs to add another little homily to his legacy. Morals make cold bed partners.

The next day, Callista struggled over the note, and finally ended with the innocuous:

"Do not worry about me. I am safe and well. I have every expectation of being there for the hell's opening, which I read about in the Courant. Congratulations!

Missing you greatly, your loving daughter, Callista."

She gave the missive to Clyde, who sealed it in a plain envelope. Callista raised an eyebrow. "You do not wish to read it?"

Clyde shrugged. "If you were to betray the master, you would have done so last night. He told me I need not read it." Clyde took the note with him.

Callista tried to peer over his shoulder to see how he opened the panel, but he was too tall.

The whole of that long day, the only activity that gave her any satisfaction was pacing. She measured the length of the vast warehouse, then the width, and finally crossed it diagonally. The scenery was beautiful but depressingly the same. She started at every sound, hoping, yet dreading, to hear Drake's steps. Her wanton behavior the night past made her blush, yet the longing to throw caution to the wind and accept his impulsive proposal was even more troubling.

Somehow they had to thrash out their conflict. Somehow she had to convince him to let her go. Before his will prevailed and her own failed.

She picked up the dressing gown he'd discarded over the settee and inhaled his scent. She clutched the soft fabric, tears coming to her eyes. Somehow she had to want to go.

When Clyde came with lunch, she demanded, "Where is Drake?"

He set the tray down without looking at her. "He asked me to tell you that he will be away for several hours. On business."

"He's a coward."

Clyde spilled the wine he was pouring for her. His long face set in what would have been, for any other man, a glare. On him it looked like he'd swallowed a lemon. "The K—Herricks are many things, but never cowardly. Has it not occurred to you that he is giving you time?"

"For what? To go mad? I have naught to do, no one to talk to—"

He gave her a mock bow.

"—save a man who should be old enough to know better than to trail around after a brigand like an adoring puppy." When he paled, Callista could have bitten off her tongue. She reached out to squeeze his arm. "Forgive me. I am cross today."

He relaxed. "You should have seen Drake last night."

His severity was lightened by the faintest smile.

Callista laughed. "Good. 'Tis his fault I hardly slept."

"Would you care to play a game of whist?"

"Only if you agree to join me for lunch. This looks delicious, thank you."

Callista waited until he was well into his meal before she said casually, "You are a man of many talents. One can only wonder how you acquired them."

Clyde paused, his fork suspended. A roasted potato plopped back on his plate. "Honestly, if that is your meaning." A wry smile stretched his lips. "At least, save for my pirate days." He stabbed a potato and bit into it savagely, as if regretting his loose tongue.

Callista pretended interest in her food. "I can hardly criticize you for that, can I? Given my ancestry, I mean."

Clyde swallowed, nodding. "Indeed. Raleigh was quite the freebooter in his day, was he not?"

"Might I ask if you served with Drake?"

Clyde hesisted, then nodded.

Feeling as if she should fetch some tongs to pry the words from him, Callista urged, "Might I ask how old he was?" She was beginning to suspect that Drake Herrick, or whatever his true name was, had acquired his survival skills at a very early age.

Clyde peered into her eyes, as if assessing her trustworthiness. "Eighteen when he began. Twenty-one when he became captain. I do not need to remind you that this information is strictly confidential."

Callista pressed a fingertip on her mouth. "Could you tell me something of that life? Truly, I only wish to understand Drake better."

Shoving his plate back, Clyde folded his arms over his breast and gave in to the inevitable. "Ah, now that was an exciting life. And me, who never wanted to be anything but a monk. Pacifism does not survive long, however, when you have a knife to your throat. I learned proficiency in all manner of weapons not by choice, but because I had to." Clyde smiled wryly. "Not that I can say the same of Drake. He took to the sword like he was born with one in his hand. A skill that saved us both more times than I care to remember."

"How did he become captain?"

"By succession. He was first mate when the captain took a cannonball from a Turkish merchant. The others were brave lads from all corners of the globe, but Drake was the only one who spoke all their languages, and he was the only true leader among them, a fact they all recognized. They gave him their confidence in their votes. He made them all rich."

"But how did he learn these skills?"

Clyde's reflective expression grew grim. "In the sultan of Turkey's prison."

Callista gasped. "But how—"

"Never mind that now. I promised Drake years ago I would never speak of those days. He will one day tell you himself, I should imagine."

Remembering the hard ridges on Drake's back, Callista was not sure she wanted to hear the details. The mere idea of how he must have suffered was enough to make her nauseous. She had to cup her stomach with both hands and force herself to listen as Clyde went on.

"To continue, 'tis amazing the skills piracy can teach one. Diplomacy, as one must deal with many different seamen from many different lands; bargaining, as one must grant terms to one's captives; trading, as one sells the captured goods; even politics, as one must continually make agreements with other pirate captains and pay tribute to the deys, sultans, and pashas of the area."

"If Drake was so good at the life, why did he leave it?"

Clyde frowned at her, as if disappointed in her dim-witted question. "There are precious few old pirates. Besides, as much as Drake tried to spare those he could, inevitably he had to kill. He did not like it, and left as soon as he had enough of a stake to buy his own merchantman. And since he knew the pirates of the area, he greased enough palms to keep them away. Thus, he sailed unmolested when all the other traders had to take their chances."

"I have observed that of him. He likes the odds best when they are in his favor." Callista sipped her wine, but it might have been prune juice, from her disapproving expression.

"And are you any different?" Clyde gripped the table to lean over it and skewer her with a gaze that had never been so sharp. "Did you not spend a hefty sum to purchase a racehorse with the best blood in the realm?"

Callista nodded, acknowledging the thrust, before she said dryly, "True. But I remind you that Drake Herrick has taken Paris from me, as well."

"Taken? Or purchased fairly?"

"I did not know my brother planned to sell my horse."

Clyde's aggressive posture softened to his usual kindness. "For that, you have my sympathy. You came here to get Paris back?"

"Such was my intent, originally." Odd, she had seldom thought of Paris in the past days. She briefly wondered if she could still challenge Drake to a game, but in truth, her heart was no longer in it.

It, too, was in peril.

"Life never seems to turn out as we expect, does it?" Clyde's eyes were gentle once again, as if he sympathized with her pain. "But you know, those odd twists and turns our road takes sometimes lead us to Elysium—if we have courage enough to dwell there rather than to pass on by."

Callista rose abruptly. "Please excuse me. Thank you for the lunch. It was quite delicious."

Odd how the catwalk twisted and turned. Upstairs Callista drew the bed curtains aside, trying to ignore the image of herself there with Drake.

Elysium? Or Hades?

She had a nagging sense that life would very soon show her the difference.

Drake patted his pocket. The reassuring crackle of paper relaxed him, but when a comely serving wench landed in his lap, he shoved her away. Her strong cologne would have, not so long ago, excited him. When she squawked, he put a sovereign in her hand. "There's another for you if you'll bring me a bottle of your best brandy and see I am not disturbed."

He'd come here resolved to end this heaviness in his loins, but damn, these wenches were common. They were too thin, or too fat, or too young, or too old.

He slugged down a full glass, coughing slightly. *Hell, I might as well admit it.* There was only one thing wrong with the serving wenches, who were known throughout London as some of the comeliest in the realm.

They were not Callista.

Even her name was pleasing to him. She was indeed "most beautiful."

Too beautiful, within and without, for a wounded

The Gentle Beast

beast such as he. Yet he could not let her go. Not now, probably not ever.

Her lie to save him had been the turning point in their relationship. She was no longer a trophy to be won or a weapon to use against Stanton.

He took another swig of his second glass to avoid putting thought to exactly what she'd become for him. The thought sneaked past the brandy's sting anyway.

In all his thirty years, she was unique. Not just for her mysterious lure, a mixture of innocence and wantonness, nor even for the acerbic wit and determination that sat so oddly on her feminine frame. She was alone among the many women he'd known in all corners of the globe for a basic reason.

She was the only woman he wanted for his wife.

And she'd made her opinion of that union abundantly clear. Apparently he was good enough to bed but not good enough to wed. He slammed the glass down so hard brandy sloshed on his waistcoat. "Maudlin fool," he growled.

The sleazy-looking individual at the next table turned to glare at him. "Is ye speakin' tae me?"

"Do I look like I addressed you, fellow?" Drake poured himself another hefty draft.

The clasp at his shoulder caught Drake by surprise. His brandy spilled again—this time on the man's hobnail boots. That full-lipped, beetle-browed face showed comical surprise, but even half drunk, Drake knew what was coming. He barely had time to get to his feet before a meaty fist aimed for his nose.

Drake dodged, catching the man about the waist and barreling him to the floor. He sensed someone behind him, and started to turn, so the blow from the hefty ale stein glanced off the side of his head. He knocked the stein away with one hand, holding the other fellow's throat with the other.

Drake felt the arm of his expensive frock coat tearing under the grasp of the man beneath him, but he was too busy kicking the other assailant's feet off balance to care. When the tall, thin man, a sailor by the looks of him, joined them on the floor, Drake used elbows, knees, and fists to land jabs where they might. He managed to dodge most of their returning blows, but when he couldn't, he absorbed the impact and kept hitting back.

The lessons he'd learned on the rat-infested docks of Bombay had come in handy before. He'd not expected to use them in one of the most respectable tap houses in England.

In two minutes flat, both his assailants were supine, pleading for mercy. Drake stood unsteadily, straightening his mask. He looked at the other patrons, but they showed an uncommon interest in their ale. Drake fluttered his torn laces over his bruised knuckles, slapped a sovereign down before the barkeep, and sauntered out.

A buzz burst out in his wake, but he scarcely heeded it. His grin was cocky as he ambled down the street. Damn, it felt good to use his hands again in something so simple as self-defense. And the minor little tumble wouldn't hurt his larger purpose, either.

Another rumor to feed the mill. The more the Dragon was feared, the better. Besides, the new *Letter of Junius* Drake had received from Wilkes's man on the street was doubtless the usual triumph of subversiveness. He'd read it later, when his knuckles had quit stinging so much.

The masculine glow of accomplishment warded off his depression. Time to face another opponent with more formidable skills. He turned toward his warehouse, resolved to force the little minx to admit she cared for him. When she did, he could admit he wanted her beyond reason and would do almost anything to win her.

Henry Stanton's gaunt face rose before his mind's eye.

Almost anything.

Drake was so caught up in his feelings that he didn't see the two men he'd trounced stagger out of the taproom. They waited until he turned a corner, then hastened after him on silent, practiced feet.

A few hours later, Callista poured Clyde another glass of claret. "A scoundrel your master may be, but one thing I'll say for him—he has excellent taste." Callista sipped appreciatively. The silence on the catwalk had left her prey to thoughts she could not bear. This company was much more felicitous.

"Indeed." Clyde held his glass up in a silent salute to her. "In all things."

Callista nodded. "Thank you. Now, your move."

They were too intent on their game to notice the click of the opening panel. Soft footsteps paused, then approached.

Clyde cocked his head to appraise the chessboard. " 'Fortune helps the brave,' " he quoted, moving out his queen.

Callista caught it with her knight. "And 'diligence is the mother of good fortune,' as my favorite author, Cervantes, would say."

Clyde looked glumly at his king, boxed into a corner behind the paltry defense of one rook and three pawns, while she'd only lost a bishop and four pawns. He set his king on its side. "Given I have already lost three games, I do not expect a miracle. I concede. I must say, Lady Raleigh, I have never seen a woman play chess as you do."

"Perhaps the set itself brings out the best in me," she said, admiring the gleam of ivory and hematite. She patted her white queen, which was the image of Elizabeth squiring her armies to defeat the Spanish.

"Or perhaps you've an affinity with Good Queen Bess," said a deep voice. "She did reject every suitor in favor of her virgin status."

Under that needling stare, Callista gave him a haughty look that Elizabeth would have been proud of.

Clyde rose hastily. "Excuse me, sir, I did not expect you until later."

" 'Tis obvious. Enjoying yourself, Clyde?" Drake came into the pool of lantern light.

Callista's eyes widened. Drake's blue velvet coat was torn, his laces dirty and bloodstained, his knuckles bruised. She rose and approached him in concern. "Are you all right?"

Clyde dipped a clean cloth in the ewer by their side and approached to wrap it about Drake's hand, but Drake shoved him away. "You know I do not like you to fuss. I am fine. A mere annoyance, which I dealt with readily enough."

Callista sniffed his jacket. Her expression lost all concern as she retook her seat. "Why do you not call a spade a spade and admit you were in a tavern brawl?"

"Indeed. And it has invigorated me for a tussle of another kind. You may go, Clyde."

Clyde glanced between the pair, opened his mouth, then shut it. He reluctantly exited.

The smell of brandy could not hide a more alluring, subtle perfume. He'd bedded some wench. Yet oddly

The Gentle Beast

he was still aroused, focused on her like a hound about to pounce on a vixen.

Callista's nape tingled in response. She turned away to wander the room, resolved that this time he would not see her weakness. "Was your companion pleasing?"

He approached, turning her gently to face him. "Not pleasing enough. She was dark, you see. Her hair couldn't warm a man, body and soul. Her charms filled my arms too full and my heart not at all." He held out his hands. Even the mask could not disguise his eagerness.

Stuffing her hands in her pockets, Callista closed her eyes. *What sins have I committed to warrant this torment? If only . . .*

She opened her eyes and lied steadily. "I find I have a distaste of dragons."

If she had only herself to think of, she'd count the world well lost and spend the rest of her life with him in this lair. Only the memory of him hovering over Henry like a vengeful spirit on that first fateful meeting kept her strong.

His hands dropped. They clenched, then relaxed under the sheer power of his formidable will. "How inconvenient for you, as it will take the might of St. George himself to keep me from you. Since you seem to be short a shield and a sword, why do you not accept the inevitable?"

"Nothing is inevitable in life but death. As for the rest, we make our own fates. You can steal my freedom, my home, my horse, and even my virtue. You can never replace my love for Henry. As long as you persecute him, you remain my enemy." The words were the hardest she'd ever spoken, but God save her, they were true.

He flinched. He reached out to grab her, but when she met him eye for eye, will for will, he turned away with a curse.

"Bah! At least the serving wench knew how to be a woman. You're a shrew who needs taming, but I've no stomach for you tonight. Leave me."

Callista forced herself to walk with dignified grace to the catwalk. Just a minute longer. Then she could pull the bed curtains and give way to the tears.

If she shed an ocean of them, perhaps she could sail away on the dreams he'd shattered. . . .

Outside, a dark carriage with the curtains drawn tight pulled up in an adjacent alley. The two men who'd followed Drake home slunk out of the shadows. The sailor bowed, his prominent Adam's apple bobbing with nervousness. "Evenin', guv."

"Well? What did you find?" Looking about, Quartermain pulled the window curtain aside enough to see his hireling.

"Only this." The man stuck a sheaf of papers through the window.

Quartermain turned up the lantern. He scowled. "You idiot! Can't you see this paper is blank?" He held it closer to the light, as if he couldn't believe his eyes. A silvery line appeared. He gasped, holding the paper before the flame. Slowly more lines took life. His grin was sharply cast above the light, his bold nose and handsome forehead lending him a saturnine mien. "Excellent! The noose tightens." He glanced sharply at his man. "Did anyone see you take this?"

"Naw, we did it while we was fightin' 'im."

"Well done. Now go back to your post until your replacement comes. The man who catches them loading the flyers gets a handsome bonus of ten quid." Quartermain whisked the curtain closed and tapped the roof. The coach swayed off, quiet because of the bags over the horses' hooves.

The full-lipped man stared after his employer. "'E's a devil, that one. Did ye see that grin?" He shuddered.

The sailor rubbed his sore midsection. "But that cursed dragon bloke deserves him. It's the ten quid wot interests me. What do ye thinks were on a blank paper to make it worth so much?"

Inside the warehouse, Drake poured himself a third glass of brandy. The ache didn't stop, but it was growing pleasantly dull. He told himself to pull out the papers and return to business, but he hadn't the energy for it. Precisely for that reason, he made himself dip his hand in his pocket.

He frowned, feeling the other side. His heart skipped a beat, then began to race. He turned both pockets inside out, but he wasn't that drunk.

The text of the new flyer was gone.

He sat back in his chair. That forced confrontation in the tavern finally made sense. "You prideful fool. Now what?"

Only the invisible ink would save him. If the two were mere pickpockets, they'd throw the blank sheaf of papers away. If they were hirelings . . .

The intuition that had saved his life on more than one occasion made his eyes go unfocused and his spine stiffen. "Damn your black soul to hell, Quartermain."

He rose to stride up and down between the settee and the fire. This he had not foreseen. The Lady Callista Raleigh could well put a period to his existence if he weren't careful. Perhaps he should release her.

"No." He gripped the back of the desk chair so hard that something snapped in his hand. He looked down.

A piece of the delicate finial had broken. Drake tossed it on the desk, stared at his writing paper, and sat down. Under the circumstances, caution was the name of the game. He unlocked a hidden compartment and dipped his quill in the invisible ink.

Fifteen minutes later, he returned to the lair and turned down the lanterns to their faintest glow. Then, with a sign of relief, he turned his back to the catwalk and removed his mask. He rubbed his tired features and stared into the fire.

One could not describe the man revealed as handsome. His nose was too sharp, his chin too bold, and his ears too large. The faded scar running down one eyebrow to his temple accented his fierce masculinity. But the eyes his father had blessed him with were so blue that they seemed a remnant of the fantasies he'd forsworn: Atlantis pools, a unicorn's lake, or, that most elusive of chimeras, true blue love. No one who'd looked into those eyes, fringed with long, curling black lashes, ever forgot them.

However, he seldom gave his unusual eyes a thought, except to curse them for making him memorable. Yet on this lonely night he'd give half he possessed to go to Callista as he was and share all with her. The strange urge to ask her advice astonished him, for he seldom discussed his options with anyone, even Clyde.

To squelch the need, he rose and went to the chess set to polish it. As he picked up the queen, a soft sound raised the hairs on the back of his neck. He went closer to the catwalk. There it was again, louder.

Dear God, she was crying. He slammed the ivory chess piece down. He'd set one foot on the stairs before he remembered his mask. He tied his mask down and bolted back up the steps. He eased through the cur-

The Gentle Beast

tains, letting his eyes grow accustomed to the dark. He groped his way to the bed and ducked under the silk hangings.

This close, her soft sobs almost tore him apart. He gritted his teeth under the reciprocal pain and bit out, "Do you hate me so much that you weep in misery at my company?"

A caught breath answered him, then a shuddery sigh. "No. At its loss. We cannot go on this way. You have to let me go."

Drake acted on instinct. He dropped to his knees beside her and fumbled for her hands. He brought them to his chest, inside his open shirt, glad of the darkness that shielded his own watery eyes. She gasped, then traced his strong torso eagerly. He made sure that she felt the scar on his side. Then he drew her hands away, kissed her palm, and said into it, "I cannot bear your tears. All I want is to see you happy, and safe. Beauty, will you marry me?"

Her eager fingers went still. When she would have withdrawn her hands, he caught them in his own.

"Do not ask me again. I cannot choose between you and Henry. If I wed you, I would one day be forced to."

The sheer torment in her voice gave him hope. "You must see that I cannot release the daughter of my enemy when she knows so much about me. But my wife—"

"All the more reason for me to say no. If I ever wed, which I shall not, it will be for one reason."

He heard the forbidden word in her tone. He could offer her material possessions, passion, and respect, but not that. "You ask more than I can give."

"I've asked naught from you. I know better than to expect feelings from a stone. Save us both some pain and let me go."

As if cued, he put her hands back on the covers and surged to his feet, hitting his head on the bedpost. He cursed. She held back a nervous giggle.

"This is not the end of it. I shall see you at breakfast." He bent for his mask and fumbled his way out.

In her self-imposed exile, Callista tossed and turned. At least her tears had dried under the fire of righteous indignation. He could not bear her tears, when he was responsible for every one of them? And how dare he allow her the tantalizing sensation of touch but not sight? And to continue to insult her with his insincere proposals, well, he was a bounder at best.

Callista was so busy shoring up her anger that the voices took a while to impinge on her consciousness.

She couldn't hear what was said, but she recognized Drake's deep tones and a softer male voice. A visitor? This was a first. Callista felt blindly for her robe, knowing she'd catch their attention if she turned up the lamp. Robed, she eased outside the drapes that covered the alcove on the catwalk. She blinked against the light, and then focused on Drake. His back was turned to her as he blocked her view of someone who must be shorter.

Callista crept down the stairs. She ducked behind a tall chest. When she was certain they had not seen her, she peeked out. She blinked and stared.

Her heart sank to her soft slippers. If she'd doubted the proof of that printing press, she couldn't any longer, for it lived and breathed before her.

She'd never seen this man in the flesh, but she recognized him from his depictions in the press.

John Wilkes, leader of the parliamentary reform movement, could be here, in Drake's hidden lair, for only one reason.

Chapter Seven

"Yes, I know the fellow," Wilkes said. "Cannot say I've ever found him interested in fealty to the Crown. Quartermain is loyal to no one but himself."

"True. But he wants a certain houseguest of mine. He'll do anything to win her, and the notoriety he'd gain from catching us would certainly not hurt his ambitions." Drake poured his guest a second glass of port. "I sent for you as soon as I realized what happened."

Wilkes sipped appreciatively, his plain features somehow arresting. He was not a tall man, or a handsome man, but he had a certain charisma that drew people—when he troubled to use it. "This necessitates a change of plan, of course. I shall rewrite the letter, and we must change our shipment date. I hate to make the flyers a week late when we are becoming so effective, but perhaps the anticipation will help our cause. Do you still think the press is safe where it's located?"

"For the moment. Unless circumstances change."

Colleen Shannon

Amusement made Wilkes almost handsome. "Ah, yes. I have heard the rumors. And where are these circumstances currently?"

When Drake merely sipped his port, Wilkes's eyes narrowed. But he didn't push. "Very well. Now, as to the next meeting. Do you plan to be . . ." He trailed off, his eyes widening, when Callista stepped boldly from her hiding place.

"Indeed. I, too, should like to know that. Do you plan to attend the next meeting of rabble-rousers, Drake?"

Wilkes's wandering gaze settled sharply on her face.

Drake hurried to her side to take her arm and urge her toward the steps. When she pulled away, standing her ground, he said, "Now, my lady, we are discussing things that do not concern you."

"I should think they concern any loyal Englishman." She nodded regally to Wilkes. "Or Englishwoman."

He recovered quickly from his surprise; she had to give him that. He came forward, his hand extended. "I have ever wanted to meet you, Miss Raleigh."

Drake glared at him, then put a finger to his lips behind Wilkes's back.

Callista ignored the hint. All of London apparently suspected she was here. Besides, Wilkes could hardly bandy the information about, given that he had so much to lose if they came to look for her. Callista gave him her fingertips, then pulled away quickly. "I would that I could say 'tis a pleasure to meet you."

He lifted an eyebrow at the rudeness. "Odd. I had been under the impression that you were an admirer of mine."

Now who had told him that? Marian, probably. "In my youth. From a more mature perspective, I can see that your tactics are not only ill advised, they could lead to dire consequences."

170

The Gentle Beast

"You look deucedly young to me, if you do not mind my saying so, child."

Enough of his condescension. "Sir, what would you do if England rallied to overthrow the Crown?"

Wilkes's smirk faded. "Why, celebrate, I should imagine."

"And what would you have us replace it with?"

He shrugged. "Some form of elected government that means something, wherein one man did not hold the power of life and death over us."

"And would women be allowed to vote?"

His mouth dropped open. "I should say not! Women are emotional creatures without the grasp of . . ." He trailed off as he finally saw the trap she'd set for him.

"Indeed. From a purely emotional perspective, you understand, Elizabeth not only held her realm together, she brought us from a second-rate power to world dominion in her lifetime. And this with Spain always hovering like a vulture. Could she have done what she did in some elective Utopia with a group of squabbling men leading England hither and yon?"

"Well, I, uh—"

"According to your vision, she would not even have been queen. I grant you that George the Third can be stubborn, putting his own interests above those of his people, but our monarchy has survived so long precisely because it has led us well. Before we replace it with 'some form of elected government' we should be certain we have the support of a majority of Englishmen—and women. And winning that cannot be done by the purveyance of secret papers distributed at midnight." Callista smiled sweetly. "Or such is the perspective I have. I am an admittedly emotional creature."

Drake smiled wryly as Wilkes finally found his

tongue. "You make telling points, I admit, but you've one flaw in your reasoning. George the Third will not allow even the discussion of such an alternative, much less its formation."

"Perhaps. But I would think a better way of effecting the change you want would be through the education of the populace."

Wilkes turned his back on her, continuing his conversation with Drake as if she had never interrupted. "We have several new converts I should like you to speak with at our next meeting. As one of the richest men in London, your support is invaluable, as I am sure you know. You are a man before your time, my dear fellow. Since we cannot speak openly without persecution, we shall act secretly until the day when men of all stations support the distribution of power. Together we shall topple this tin Teutonic tyrant. . . ."

Callista sat down, grimly aware that her little lecture had done no good. Still, by the time Wilkes left a few minutes later, still ignoring her, she was not sorry she had spoken. At least seeing the man face-to-face had cured her of her own infatuation with him. When Drake returned from seeing Wilkes out, Callista asked bluntly, "Can you not see what an opportunist that man is?"

Drake leaned against a chest, his strong legs crossed. "So are we all, in one way or another. Did you not come here seeking an opportunity to retrieve your horse?"

Clyde must have told him. "Yes. But I planned to give you your money back and challenge you to a game, not steal him, as you seem to imply."

"Challenge me, eh?" He straightened and approached. "Come then. Give me your best."

Callista rose. "I think not. I have seen the way you react when you are challenged. Nor do I ask for Paris back any longer. I shall not give you the satisfaction of denying me."

He still approached. "How do you know I can deny you anything?"

Callista ducked behind a table. "I would rather discuss your alliance with Wilkes. Can you not see that the cause that matters most to John Wilkes is John Wilkes?"

Drake shrugged. "So? Again, he is no different from the rest of us."

"I beg to differ. If he pushed for parliamentary reform openly, honestly, I could join him, but this subversive nastiness will do naught but stir up more trouble. If you do not end your alliance with him, you will end on Tyburn."

Drake's gaze flickered at the mention of the famous hanging hill outside London. "If it is known I kidnapped you, I could well end there anyway."

Callista turned away, unable to bear the fruitless argument any longer. Damn him. She'd proved she could hold her tongue. But this foolishness with Wilkes would be his undoing if he did not desist. And she could be undone with him if she were not careful. "You are stubborn beyond belief. I bid you good night."

He took a step toward her, hand extended, but she ignored him. His bit-off curse as he stomped away to a dark corner should have made her feel better.

It didn't.

Nor did the too soft bed and the too comfortable pillow. She tossed and turned for over an hour, wondering what to do. Her life was complicated enough without this constant choice between the fire and the frying pan. Through tragedy and triumph, wealth and want, the Raleighs had maintained loyalty to the Crown, even when it led to their own death or dishonor. George III was indeed a tyrant, an increasingly irrational one, but change should come in the courts and Parliament, not in back alleys.

Dress it up as she might, Drake Herrick was a traitor. What in heaven's name was she to do about it?

The next morning, Callista arose heavy eyed from lack of sleep. She'd struggled with her dilemma the night through, but finally she stared at herself in the mirror and faced the truth.

It must be the Raleigh lot in life to choose consorts unwisely. Her illustrious ancestor Sir Walter had himself lost Queen Elizabeth's favor when he wed one of her court ladies. Later he lost his head to a jealous, insecure James I because of his bold independence and revered standing among the English people. Yet, knowing his life was forfeit, he returned from his last doomed expedition to search for Coronado, the city of gold, and cheerfully met his execution rather than forsake the land he loved.

If she persisted in this attachment, she could well meet the same fate, but it seemed the choice was no longer hers. Loyalty to England paled beside her emotional attachment to this wounded beast. He needed her, whether he knew it or not.

His downfall would not come at her hands. Still, when the authorities caught up with Wilkes, as they surely would, they'd catch Drake also.

Callista closed her eyes in pain, but she clenched her fists so hard that her nails drew blood. When her eyes opened, they were as green as jade, and equally hard.

She didn't have to be here to see it. Somehow she'd find a way out of this luxurious prison.

She marched to the armoire and drew out the burgundy velvet day gown with sable trim at the low bosom and tight sleeves. Deliberately she left off the usual petticoat so that the fabric hugged her curves. Pearl buttons marched down the back and adorned the sleeves. She twisted and turned, buttoning them as best she could. She hesitated; then she brushed her hair and left it loose. It fell past her waist, a rippling fire that danced with every shade of red as her head turned. The heavy waves complemented the color of the gown.

She seldom used her attributes so blatantly, but she feared he'd see desperation in her eyes. She'd give him something else to think about.

She hurried downstairs to begin her search.

Outside, Drake hunkered down with Clyde behind a dray. Sure enough, two men loitered about, stamping their feet and blowing into their hands against the cold. He didn't recognize them, but he knew who'd sent them.

He ducked back around, saying to Clyde, "When our bait arrives and they leave their post, come get me and we'll take the shipment then."

"Very well, sir. But I have not had time to prepare breakfast yet."

"I can manage. Our guest will have to make do with tea and day-old scones." Drake strode back into his shop.

Later he scowled as he climbed down the stairs, feeling awkward with the unaccustomed tray. Hellfire and damnation, this woman had caused him nothing but trouble since he first laid eyes on her. Now she had Quartermain breathing down his neck like a randy stallion.

The last thing he needed was more enemies. His combative thoughts fled as he closed the panel behind

175

him and saw her. He blinked. His heartbeat accelerated as, for the second time, he saw her with her hair loose. She sat in front of the fire, holding the heavy mass of living flame to one side as she brushed it. She leaned slightly forward, so her breasts pressed against the low bodice. One long leg was extended before her, bare to the knee.

The velvet and fur emphasized the richness of her lush beauty. Why had she dressed so seductively? he wondered with a last grasp on reason. He fumbled to set the tray down as it tilted in his hands.

Then blood rushed to the aching center of his body. He could not think; he could not speak; he could not even move.

Forward was disaster and backward was beyond him.

Thus he stood frozen in sheer torment, wondering vaguely what he'd done to deserve this continual arousal without relief. Even the torture he'd suffered as a young man could not compare to this. She leaned forward, her breasts almost falling free; then that exquisite expanse of flesh was covered as she flipped her hair over her head to brush it downward.

He wanted to go warm his hands on her, but he'd felt the proof of her virtue himself. Even to hurt Henry Stanton he could not take this beauty without all the laws of God and man sanctifying their union. Or so he told himself, finally closing his eyes to deny temptation. It didn't help. Vivid memories of what her bare torso looked like, and felt like, hardened him to a state that could have but one end.

Before he could stop himself, he took two steps toward her. She stopped brushing, flipped her hair to one side, and peered at him with one inscrutable green eye. He'd have given the contents of this warehouse to know her thoughts, but she merely flipped her hair back over and continued brushing.

He covered the remaining distance between them quickly. He pulled the brush away and tilted her chin up, his other hand buried in the vital warmth of her flowing mane. "You look too lovely already. Have done, I pray you, else I may eat *you* for breakfast."

"And you might chip a tooth. I am tougher than I look." But she rose and followed him to the tray set on a carved wooden table.

He pulled out her chair. When she sat down, her breasts squeezed together in a bounteous display that did indeed make him ravenous. He turned away to adjust his aching privates in his breeches. Then, a smile pasted beneath his scarlet mask, he sat down opposite her, as far away as he could get.

She raised an eyebrow, but merely buttered a scone and smeared it with jam. "What mission is Clyde on this morn?"

He froze, his teacup halfway to his mouth. "How do you know he's, er, on a mission?"

"He even looks like your faithful hound. He is never far from your side, unless he is hurrying about your bidding. Care to tell me what you have done to inspire such loyalty? I know you saved his life, but he would tell me little else—save that you were a most skilled pirate. An attribute that does not surprise me." She looked at him sidelong.

Drake was glad of the mask: The minx was too intelligent for her own good. "You did well to wheedle that much out of him. May I suggest that you mind your own business? 'Twould be safer."

She daintily wiped her mouth. "For me or for you?"

"For both of us," he said grimly.

"You speak as if our fates are irrevocably bound. We are not a couple."

"Yet." He stared at her until she lifted her downcast face, but she looked away before he could read her expression.

She shoved her half-eaten scone away. Something was obviously bothering her. "Forgive me, I am a bit uncertain of the proper rules of behavior between prisoner and gaoler, but I should imagine they have no common ground but the same cell."

"Very well, I shall." With measured precision, he folded his napkin beside his empty plate. When she looked confused, he added, "Forgive you." He surged to his feet and shouted, "For your cursed stubbornness, your obtuseness, and, and . . ." He trailed off and sat back down. "But most of all I forgive your come-hither, go-away smile that is driving me mad."

This time she didn't look away. "Then God pity us both, for that is the way you make me feel. I do not know whether to hold you close or run screaming from a man who will not even show me his face."

For the first time he noticed the circles under her eyes. He felt a twinge of pain at the knowledge that he had likely caused them. "Then let me make your life simpler."

He rose, rounded the table, and did something then that no force on earth had ever made him do: he bent on one knee before her. Holding one of her clammy hands, he said softly, "Beauty, will you marry me?"

She looked down, trying to pull away. He rubbed her hand between his own, warming it. "I shall ask you every day until you say yes out of sheer exhaustion. Come now, just one three-letter word and we can both rest."

She laughed but said, "A two-letter word will have to

The Gentle Beast

do. No. Now get up. With that fearsome mask, you look ridiculous."

He stood, only to grab her hands and ease her up with him. "Why not?"

She pulled away and strode up and down, as if she could not keep still. "I confess that if you had not made my life so cursed complicated, I might consider your suit in all seriousness."

He caught his breath and took a giant step toward her, stopping only when she raised her hand.

"But you have, even more after last night."

He frowned. "Last night? But we barely spoke."

"Indeed. But I had a most interesting conversation with your visitor."

"Wilkes."

"Yes. And while I have, on occasion, felt great sympathy with his ideals, I cannot support his actions. If you have thrown in your lot with Wilkes, I can never throw in my lot with you. Many things the Raleighs have been over the years, but I will not be the first of the line to support outright insurrection against the Crown."

Drake sat down sideways in the chair. Indeed, this did tangle their coil into a veritable knot. He rested an elbow on the chair back and propped his chin in his hand. "Why did you admit this? Do you not realize it gives me even more reason to hold you?"

It seemed she wouldn't reply, and then she said so softly that he had to strain to hear, "So that when I leave, you will know that, despite everything, I will not betray you."

He closed his eyes in pain. "Do not speak of leaving me."

"Very well then. What shall we speak of?"

He rose to escort her to the sofa. When her skirts

were prettily arranged, he made to sit beside her, looked at the fairy-tale beauty his heart desired, and wisely chose the chair opposite. "We seem to be good at pretense. Shall we pretend we are at tea, in the marchioness's salon, arguing the finer points of liberty as every good subject does?" He made to pick up an imaginary china cup, holding it primly in one large hand, his pinky comically extended.

Her soft laugh delighted him. Maybe they could discuss the explosive subject calmly.

Some of the tension eased from her face. She pretended to pour herself a cup of tea, added sugar from dainty tongs, and stirred. "So what think you of the *Letters of Junius*, m'lord?"

He started at the title, then calmed when he realized she had thrown herself into her role with vigor. "They are a much-needed voice of opposition to tyranny. The masses can be subjected to oppression only so long before outright rebellion effects what Parliament will not. I support John Wilkes for this reason only. I do not always agree with what he writes, but given that his duly elected seat in the Commons was thrice stolen from him, I certainly support his right to espouse his discontent."

If she had really held a teacup, she would have spilled the brew in her lap. "Every good Englishman takes the scurrilous writings for what they are: treason."

He would have crushed a cup, had he held one. "One man's treason is another's liberty. Tell me, dear lady, have you followed the unrest in the colonies?"

"Somewhat. But I often wonder if we truly get the right of it in the papers here."

"You do not. I have visited the colonies frequently over the years and was in fact present when a young

The Gentle Beast

Virginian by the name of Patrick Henry gave a speech in the House of Burgesses, Williamsburg, Virginia, which I shall never forget. He said, 'Caesar had his Brutus; Charles the First, his Cromwell; and George the Third—*may profit by their example.* If *this* be treason, make the most of it.' "

She folded her arms over herself, as if chilled. "Are you suggesting that we kill the king?"

"Of course not. Only pointing out that here such words are treason, but in America many, save the most ardent Tories, revere young Henry as a patriot. And those of your set may consider the *Letters of Junius* scurrilous, but I tell you that among the costermongers, tavern-keepers, and sailors, those who can read do so with enthusiasm, and those who cannot beg that the next flyer be read to them. I merely want reform to come peacefully, before unrest comes here as it has to the colonies. Mark this: that massacre in Boston a couple of years back is the start of armed insurrection unless the king eases his iron yoke."

"But we are his subjects, bound by centuries of tradition to follow his edicts."

"Straight to disaster? There is something wrong with a system of government whereby a poor child can be whipped to work from dawn till dusk, and a poor girl can be kidnapped and sold to a brothel, both without hope of rescue. Do the same to a rich child, or girl, and all the laws of the land will seek out their defilers and clap them in irons. Is this your idea of justice?"

She worried the sable trim on her sleeve. She bit her lip, then shook her head. "I confess I have often thought the same. But what are we to do to change things?"

Drake stood. "That, my dear girl, is the difference between us. You think; I act."

She flinched. Drake sighed and lowered his voice. "Forgive me. Had I lived your sheltered existence, I would probably feel the same. But I know how ruthless the world is to those without money or power. Now that I have both, I will use them as my conscience dictates to better the lot of those who have neither. If this means I dance at the end of a rope, so be it."

"So be it." She rose to face him. "My convictions may not be as strong as yours, but one thing I understand better than you: anger begets anger, hatred more hatred. Violent opposition will make the king more stubborn. Only the will of all the English people, rich and poor alike, will be strong enough to redress the injustices you cite, and many others. And the *Letters of Junius* are alienating those who must lead the fight. Now please excuse me, but I wish some privacy."

Whisking her skirts aside from him, she climbed the stairs with measured dignity. As usual he was left watching her leave, feeling the fool. When she closed the curtains over the alcove, he was galvanized. Damn her, she could never shut him out. He strode after her, caught himself, and spun the other way. He had to get out of here before he did something he might regret.

He was too angry to hear the slight rattle as the drapes were pulled aside, or to notice the spyglass that poked an inquisitive eye through the heavy velvet. Drake pushed three curlicues on the wall panel simultaneously, and it slid open. He slammed it shut.

The spyglass withdrew. Angry footsteps retreated; then all was silent, save for the crackling of the fire and a soft whisper of grief.

Callista hugged the pillow tightly, trying to get energy enough to rise. All had been silent for a good half hour, so it should be safe to leave.

The Gentle Beast

Tears welled up again, and simply because the thought of leaving him gave her such misery, she forced herself to get up. She looked at the chest of clothes he'd given her, but knew she could not take them. They would be as stolen as this time with him. She needed no reminders to bring back memories that would haunt her always. Drake holding her, kissing her, teasing her, asking her to marry him. In another reality they could have been so happy together. But she could only make the best of the reality God had given her.

"You ninny, you'd best flee while you can." The sound of her own voice, soft and husky with tears, disgusted her so that she stood. She wiped her tears on the soft cloth beside the basin, poured herself a glass of water, and drank.

Then, picking up the spyglass so she could return it to its hidden panel in the liquor cabinet, she descended the stairs. She'd just replaced the exquisite little thing when she heard an astounding sound. Her mouth dropped open.

A carriage? Here? She looked toward the warehouse rear. A screeching noise was followed by a crack of light that grew wider as the noise grew louder. She was so accustomed to the dimness of this vast warehouse that she'd forgotten it must have a rear cargo door.

The gap became a square opening tall enough for a dray and a team of workhorses. Drake himself pulled the wagon up. He and Clyde alighted and closed the wide door. Boards rattled, and then the two men pulled out the floor of the wagon and stacked the planks against the wall. Drake opened the secret storage closet. They began loading leaflets into the space beneath the wagon's floorboards.

Callista eyed the chain that opened the door. More

fool she for never noticing it, not that she'd be able to move it alone, but Drake kept a wary eye on her. She knew he almost wished she'd try to bolt. Instead she sauntered over and glanced inside the wagon. She was surprised at the hidden space. She pulled back to eye the sideboards.

Really, they looked too narrow from the sides to hide anything. She stooped and looked beneath. Only then could one see that the real floor of the wagon was a good foot under the side supports, built at an angle to be even more inconspicuous.

She straightened. "So I can add smuggling to your other sins."

He dropped a heavy load of leaflets inside as if they weighed nothing. "Indeed, and the list seems to grow every time I am near you."

She reared back. "Do not blame me for your own shortcomings."

He growled. "I agree, my comings have certainly not been short since I met you. Indeed, I've had none at all."

When she stared at him blankly, he turned away with a curse. Callista wondered why Clyde turned beet red and hung his head.

She flounced off. "Well, let me remove my irksome presence." But she found a seat close enough to see and hear what went on.

They made short work of the rest of the leaflets. When they were ready to leave they stacked heavy furniture on top of the fake floorboard. Clyde hopped back on the wagon seat.

"Remember the code?" Drake asked.

Clyde nodded.

"I shall make sure they're still . . . occupied." Drake opened the door, his muscles a fluid ballet under his shirt as he heaved on the heavy chain. He disappeared outside but returned shortly. "All's clear. Be sure you pay the girls two guineas each." Clyde turned the wagon about with great skill in the cramped space; then he clucked to the horses.

Callista's eyes narrowed. No doubt they'd hired whores to distract whoever watched the warehouse. *How typical.*

The rattle of chain came again; then the warehouse seemed dimmer than before. Mournfully Callista watched the light go out. When the source of her darkness came to the ewer to wash his hands, she lashed out at him.

"You really are a scoundrel. Do you always hire strumpets to do your dirty work?" She turned up the lantern at her side.

He paused in soaping his hands, then rubbed them together harshly. "I do what the task requires. I suggest you remember that. And by the by, they were glad to get ten times their usual rate. You should know first-hand that I am no corrupter of innocents." He glanced over his shoulder. The lamp cast wicked shadows on the mask. "Push me further, and I may add that to my list of sins."

She bristled. "Empty threats do not alarm me. If you were to have your wicked way with me you'd have done so by now."

A tense, beating silence; then, with a whoosh that might have been his clothes rubbing together, he was upon her. He seemed giant against the shadows, his broad shoulders dragon wings that could either protect her or consume her, at his whim.

"Do not taunt me. I cannot sleep, I cannot eat, I can barely think for wanting you. If you doubt it . . ." He caught her hand and forced it to the bulge in the front

Colleen Shannon

of his breeches. She tried to pull away, but he held her there in the intimate pose until their breathing quickened. "After so long without release, it becomes painful for a man. You are a temptress, for, as God is my witness, no other woman will do."

Callista closed her eyes, but the feel of him, so full and needful, was a temptation greater than any Eve must have faced. She tried to pull away, but he only held her tighter. His breath, hot with a similar need, blasted the nape of her neck. Any second now her hand would betray her with the urge to touch him, to know him as they both wanted.

Just when she thought she'd scream, he released her. His breathing ragged, he retreated to the shadows like a wounded beast. She felt him watching her, so she struggled to compose herself.

When she could control her voice, she said, "Then let me go if I cause you such distress."

A harsh laugh blasted out of the murk like a volley of gunfire. "'Tis too late for that. I've no notion to spend the rest of my days in gaol. You back me into a corner, my beauty. You will not wed me, you will not bed me. Yet this dread of me is patently false. You wanted to touch me just then as badly as I want to touch you. I shall thus hold you until you change your mind. Marry me, and you are free—as long as you come back to me."

"I will never be free of you," she whispered, too soft for him to hear.

"What's that?"

She rose. "'Tis of no importance. If you will excuse me, I have the headache." She gave him a wide berth, but she felt his urge to reach out and conquer. One step, two—she was almost at the stairs. Then came the scrape of a chair grinding backward, and a muffled

186

curse. She heard his angry footsteps approach the sideboard, and the clink of bottle against glass.

Damn you, do your drinking in a tavern so I can flee as I should have days ago.

Her measured steps successfully hid her tormoil. Finally she reached the alcove. Lonely sanctuary, perhaps, but 'twas obvious he would never give up his vengeance against Henry. They could be nothing to each other, least of all husband and wife.

She lectured herself for the next half hour, listening for the soft snap of the panel opening and closing. It did not come, and her lecture to herself only made her more miserable.

As Clyde Haynes rounded the corner toward the delivery site a few streets over, he saw Quartermain and the magistrate. He checked the workhorses reflexively, then eased the reins, forcing the panic from his face. When both men pulled their lathered horses in front of him he was forced to stop. "Yes, gentlemen, may I help you?"

The magistrate, a portly man in a waistcoat, opened his mouth, but Quartermain beat him to it. "Nice try, Haynes. You can tell your devil of a master that he may dupe my men with his sleazy little trick, but I am made of sterner stuff. Get down so we can search the wagon." Quartermain dismounted.

"And why, pray, should I do that?"

"Because I bring formal charges against you and your master in the morning. On the small matter of treason, in publishing and propagating the *Letters of Junius.*"

Clyde's long face settled into a look of amusement. "Is that so? Well, in that case, search all you wish." He got down.

Colleen Shannon

The magistrate glared at the cit, but the little man was obviously accustomed to the foibles of the quality. Clyde opened his mouth to disabuse the poor man that Quartermain could ever be considered such. Then, shrugging, Clyde climbed down, holding the horses while he waited to see what the magistrate would do.

The official hesitated. Then he snorted in concert with his fat horse. He dismounted, wheezing with the effort, and waddled over to assist Quartermain in banging through dresser doors and desks, and fumbling through cushions.

A crowd had gathered to watch. In other circumstances, Clyde would have been amused at their asides.

"Cor, if ye finds a quid or two in them sofas, it belongs to me!" said a mousy-looking youth with the quick hands and feet of a pickpocket.

A fat washerwoman laughed, her reddened hands and stained apron testimony to her occupation. "Ye'll fights me for it! I cleaned the pants wot lost it, I did!"

The crowd laughed uproariously. The magistrate paused in his search, glancing uneasily at the ring of avid faces. Quartermain didn't even look up. *He's a cool bastard, right enough,* Clyde decided. *Let's see how long he stays cool.* Clyde bestowed a friendly smile and a wink on the crowd.

"Keep the quid, sir," cried a blacksmith, his leather apron singed, his arms bulging even under his coarse shirt. "Ye'll needs it onct the fine cove is done wi' ye."

Normally Clyde would have disdained the class warfare, but these circumstances were not normal, even in his adventurous existence. If they continued shoving the furniture around, they might dislodge a board.

"Truer words were never spoken," Clyde agreed. "I am just a man working to make a living, as you are. And if I am much later in my delivery, I may be turned

The Gentle Beast

off without a reference." He made a show of opening his pocket watch, sighing his worry as he read the time.

The blacksmith scowled and caught Quartermain by the collar. "What ye lookin' for, anyways?"

Quartermain was tall enough to look the blacksmith in the eye, but he could not match him in bulk. Still, he fearlessly brushed the man's rough hand away. "None of your business, fellow, but I have reason to believe this man is delivering some of those scurrilous *Letters of Junius!*"

The magistrate paled and glanced uneasily at Quartermain, waving a hand to shush him, but the cit didn't even notice.

Those on the edge of the crowd who'd begun to drift away stopped cold and turned back. The whispers began, growing in volume as Quartermain turned away to shove a heavy washstand aside so he could appraise the floorboards.

"*Letters of Junius!* Ain't read one in a while," said the washerwoman. Others looked at her enviously. She could read? "Me da were a preacher. He taught me so's I could read the Good Book."

"Let him go. We needs every word o' trufe, God's life we does," growled the blacksmith.

"Can I haves one if ye finds 'um? I'll get me girl to read it fer me," said the little pickpocket.

The magistrate puffed up his fat torso. "Now see here, we're about the king's business, so you fellows be about your own."

The blacksmith's scowl lowered until he looked like a bull about to charge. "Don't no one gives me orders, even the ruddy king hisself. I owns me own shop not 'cause o' him, but spite o' him, with his taxes. I says, let the man be on his way. Someat us who ain't king or quality has to earn a livin'."

Colleen Shannon

A chorus of agreement swept the crowd. They began to press closer against the wagon and the men searching it. Quartermain, in the process of tapping the floorboards, fell against the wagon as he was jostled.

He turned, his gimlet blue gaze hardening on the blacksmith. "Be gone with you, then, and continue fleecing whatever fools you serve."

The magistrate's eyes darted from angry face to angry face. When the blacksmith clenched meaty fists and lowered his head on his shoulders, preparing to charge, the magistrate held up his hands. "Quiet! Or I'll have every man jack of you carted to Newgate for insurrection!"

"'Tis about time you spoke up," said Quartermain.

"You were speaking more than enough for the both of us," the man retorted.

Clyde covered a smile with his hand. The pickpocket melted into the crowd, and was followed by the more prudent among them. However, the blacksmith, the butcher, and the washerwoman remained, glaring with equal contempt at the magistrate and Quartermain.

The magistrate's voice softened as his speech patterns grew more common. "I be a working man, too. Please, go on about your business and let me do mine. We ain't found nothing, so this man will be allowed to continue."

Quartermain opened his mouth, but this time the magistrate sent him a fierce look. Quartermain snapped his mouth closed, folded his arms, and leaned against the wagon.

Clyde was dismayed to see a board shift slightly, but Quartermain's back was to it.

"So ye says," the blacksmith grumbled. But he stood back and aped Quartermain's imperious, waiting attitude, arms folded, expression black. The washer-woman went on about her business. The butcher hesitated; then he, too, hurried on his way.

The magistrate bent a stern look at Clyde. "Tell your master we are scouring London for the author of these foul lies. Woe betide him if he is involved." He grabbed Quartermain's arm and dragged him to where the horses were tethered.

While they were turned away, Clyde shifted the board back in place under the pretense of balancing his load. He finished just in time, for Quartermain rode his horse up to the wagon and leaned forward, speaking softly so the blacksmith couldn't hear. "Tell the Dragon that his diversionary tactics will not protect him long. He's chosen the wrong adversary this time. I meet fire with fire."

That gimlet gaze drew sparks off Clyde's blue-gray eyes. "And so, sirrah, does he. And I opine that he's far more used to being burned than are you." He swung up into the wagon, nodding his thanks at the blacksmith. The burly man touched his cap and swaggered down the street, apron swinging.

The magistrate and Quartermain dogged Clyde's trail, so he went past his stop and wove deeper into the rabbit warren of Whitefriars. The two men, on prime bloods, were not common sights here. As Clyde had suspected, the magistrate grew increasingly uneasy at the attention they aroused. Eyes watched from squalid shacks, and screams came once from a man as another man beat him up. The open sewer ran with rats.

The magistrate looked around uneasily, using his crop on each encroaching hand that tried to grab his bridle. Few peace officers ever ventured here without a full dragoon company to back them. Clyde had counted on the magistrate ceding ambition to common sense. When a bully staggered out of a tavern, clutching a bottle of the opiate of the masses—blue ruin— the magistrate had to rear his horse to avoid him, almost unseating himself. He growled something to Quartermain, wheeled about, and trotted away.

Quartermain kept up the chase until a harlot, one sagging breast flopping out of her filthy gown, caught his booted foot. "Wants a little excitement, guv?"

Quartermain shoved her away. She fell on her scrawny butt, raising a fist to screech obscenities at him. With a last grim look at his quarry, Quartermain gave up the chase and beat a hasty retreat.

Still, Clyde drove around for another hour before he finally approached his true destination, close by in the trading district. When he gave the voice code of "Time is on our side," the innocuous little furniture store became a haven with a gaping door. Within an hour, gladly relieved of his cargo, he was on his way back to Herrick Importers, Ltd.

Dark had descended an hour past. This part of London was never safe, especially at this time of day. Clyde had traveled far seedier ports in odd corners of the globe. Still, he started at every shadow and listened alertly for every noise. For some reason his nerves were on edge.

When the attack came, it came from above. Two men jumped into his wagon from an overhang and clubbed him to his knees. One took the reins; the other tied Clyde and shoved him prone in the empty wagon.

Then they wheeled the wagon back around toward Whitefriars.

When the sun lowered in the sky, Callista couldn't bear it any longer. As the day grew long and her nerves grew short, she'd listened to the sound of bottle scrap-

The Gentle Beast

ing against glass. She'd tried to tell herself it was best this way, that when he was roaring drunk she could escape.

But no amount of common sense could prevail over her foolish whims. She could not bear for their last evening together to end thus. Finally Callista brushed her hair back into a demure snood, straightened her white cuffs, and sought out her wounded dragon.

It was pitch dark below save for the embers in the fireplace. She bumped into a table and stopped to rub her knee. His voice came, so close that she started.

"If you know what is good for you, you shall get your enticing little butt back upstairs and usurp my bed."

"I shall gladly let you have it. Those dragon wings above me are not conducive to rest."

"The bed was not designed for rest. Shall I show you why I had it built?"

Callista blushed in the darkness. She wavered, torn between the urge to soothe and the instinct to run. As usual, he forced the choice upon her by the simple expedient of grabbing her about the waist and hauling her onto his lap. She gasped, reaching out to hold him away—until her palms touched soft hair and felt the pounding of the beating heart beneath. His shirt was open.

The thudding accelerated at her touch, proving that he was human, after all. On this last night of what might have been, couldn't she pretend that he was her husband? They had no need of physical or even mental masks. Callista melted against him. With a sigh that might have signified either victory or defeat, she wrapped her arms about his neck and touched her cheek to his.

She started, then put one hesitant hand on his bare jaw. He was not wearing the mask. He wanted her badly enough to hold her in spite of it. Moved, she felt with her fingers, his features forming behind her closed eyes.

Strong jaw, a faint stubble showing a masculine man who had to shave often. Long blade of a nose, with a slight bump that signified a break sometime in the past. Large eyes, with long, soft, curling lashes. Slim brows that slashed downward like daggers. A short scar on one temple. And the lips, ah, the lips that stole her sanity were surely as well shaped and soft as her own. Callista's own eyes grew wet at his total stillness, for she knew this trust came too late.

She shoved the thought away and traced his eyes again, feeling them close at her touch. His grip tightened, but he didn't speak. "What color?" She scarce recognized her own voice.

His was equally husky. "Blue."

"True blue. Like your heart." Callista kissed the pulse beating in his throat.

A harsh groan was torn from him. The sound held such an agony of need that Callista could only tilt her head back to meet it. There in the secret darkness where dreams are born, for the first and only time, they met halfway. And in that touch of lips to lips and heart to heart, fairy tales could come true.

If they let them . . .

Conflicts were forgotten in the sheer joy of the flesh. This time it was she who teased his lips open with her tongue, delving inside as if to learn all his secrets. He delighted in her new boldness. Following her lead, he tilted his head at her pressure so she could slant her mouth better over his. For endless moments they kissed, not giving or taking, only sharing.

Trembling, his chest heaving like a bellows, he broke the pressure and buried his lips in the sweet curve of her neck. He ripped the snood away and wrapped her hair about his fist. Then she felt his tense muscles slowly, painfully relax. His hand slipped away from her hair. He sat her upright on his lap. "Leave me now, or soon you will not be able to."

Her eyes widened. How could he know? Then she realized he meant that she should seek haven upstairs.

Lying back against his pounding heart, Callista gave him a wordless but expressive reply—she opened her mouth to him as she longed to open her body. If he had put her on the settee and taken her then, she would have welcomed him.

Drake kissed her with such gentleness that her incipient tears became a stream. His wounded hand cupped her cheek, froze. His finger traced her tears. "Why do you cry?"

Cry? These were only the beginning. Nor could she tell him that she grieved for these stolen moments that would never come again. She pulled the thong from his hair and buried her fingers in the raven mass. "It matters naught. Kiss me as if there is no tomorrow." She pulled his head down.

He resisted, but when the tip of her tongue licked the corner of his mouth, then her teeth sampled the same place, he shuddered. For the first time he became the aggressor, all male, aroused beyond reason. He draped her over his arm like an houri. On some primitive level she understood that it was he who was enslaved to her.

Power was heady. And for once she was in control, not he.

Why, then, did her own excitement grow? He unbuttoned her dress and pulled her shift down to bare her breasts. The sensitive tips touched the hair on his chest. They both groaned at the contact. She shifted her torso, her nipples becoming hard, stabbing at him. Something even harder poked at her hips, and the next thing she knew she was on her feet, being dragged toward the stairs. He gave her a shove.

"Dress for me in the white gown. I bought it thinking how you would look in my bed."

She could not see him, but that voice, both a growl and a plea, spurred her upward. She quieted the restless fears.

Just for tonight, she would live for the moment.

She would never wed, so it mattered not.

So she told herself as she undressed with shaky hands. She pulled the scandalous veil of lace over her head. Then, her heart beating like a wild thing, she lay down on the magnificent red spread, arranging herself artfully.

His slow, measured steps drew near, as if he gave her time to change her mind. She turned up the dim lantern, eager to see his face. His head topped the steps. . . .

Her heart lurched, then settled like a lump in her breast.

He was masked. It was a new mask, smiling, gentle, a sapphire blue velvet to match his luxurious robe, but still a shield between them.

She turned her head aside, suddenly shamed by the eager sweep of his gaze. She felt the bed depress as he sat beside her. She tried to pull away, but he pushed her gently back, looking his fill.

"Ah, Callista, if you knew how long I've dreamed of seeing you thus, how beautiful you are, all ivory and fire against the red covers." His hand traced the lissome curves of her body, from her arm, down her tiny waist, to her hip and leg. "Perfect. No man will ever know you but me."

The Gentle Beast

The possessiveness further shook the lovely dream. Any moment it would shatter, leaving her bleeding and torn beyond healing. She stayed still, her eyes closed, which he obviously took for shyness. He bent to give her a gentle kiss. Her lips trembled under his, arousing him even more.

He bent her over his arm, his breath hot on her bare skin. "Ever more will I remember this moment," he whispered into the fragrant vee of skin above her bodice. "Finally you are truly mine." He pulled her up and guided her to the mirror in the armoire.

"Come, darling, I have something to give you." She felt him fumble in his pocket; then a slim gold chain appeared in his hand. A brilliant flash of golden fire caught the dim light. He set an exquisite stone about her neck, a jewel she could have recognized in the darkness by touch and weight.

He gave her the Yellow Rose. Not as a sign of devotion, but as a sign of possession. She barely heard his next words through the sick pounding of her heart. "I give you this to pledge my troth. I vow that our wedding night only comes one day early. Tomorrow we wed by special license."

Callista was mesmerized by the necklace. He'd had the large stone simply set, surrounded by small, perfect white diamonds. Even in the muted light, the jewel men had died for sparkled. Callista touched it. Henry had always promised that one day it would be hers, never dreaming that another man would give it to her in a new guise.

That man made no false protestations of love. But his hands were clumsy as he attached the delicate chain, and she could not doubt his eagerness. The stone settled between her breasts, cold and hard.

It was a lodestone about her neck, a symbol of all

that he was. Hard, closed, surrounded by beautiful things, reflecting back the light rather than becoming one with it.

With this gift, his victory over her was final. He expected her to give him the last thing he had not taken, while he would not even bare his face.

However, one thing she held even more dear than her virginity—her self-respect. He was too devious to rip her gown away and lunge for her. He only rubbed her shoulders gently, despite the fact that she showed such a shameful expanse of flesh to a man who was not her husband. Damn him, he would no longer use those strong hands and their cursed gentleness against her.

Slipping lightly away, she said, "Most kind of you, sir, but I have enough jewelry." She struggled to undo the clasp.

He stayed where he was, but she sensed his frown by the downturn of that expressive mouth. "Do you not understand that I give you back your family heirloom as a pledge between us?"

"Give me what you stole? Forgive me if gratitude is beyond me." The damn thing wouldn't come undone.

Now he was ominously still. "I did not ask for gratitude."

"What do you ask of me, then? I declare I do not know."

A big hand waved in the air, but finally he shook his head as if no words came close to expressing his disappointment. "I was not asking anything. I was giving. If you cannot see that, 'tis hopeless."

Callista jerked the necklace off, breaking the fragile clasp, glad of the pain that kept her tears at bay. "Indeed, you have made it so." She tossed the necklace at him. "Keep it, to go with all your other hoarded treasures. See how much joy they give you."

He caught it. She watched him crush it so hard in his hand that the sharp facets must have torn his palm. Blood dripped between his tightly closed fingers.

She turned away so she didn't have to see his pain. She had enough of her own to deal with. Stifling a sob by sheer dint of will, she said, "Leave me. I want nothing of you. Not now, not ever."

His robe rustled. She felt him span the gap between them in two steps; then he hovered over her, his shadow huge on the wall. The dragon mask and the heavy robe did indeed make him seem a beast ready to consume her. Then his shoulders raised. In a lesser man, she might have thought his sigh a caught breath of grief.

His steps retreated, heavier than usual.

Call him back! No, flee while you can! She bit her knuckles so hard that blood dotted the skin, but she scarcely noticed it through the searing pain in her heart. What folly, to spoil the dreams she might have carried away.

But that stone, and the mask he still wore, rammed the truth unpleasantly home. Pretend though she might, the reality was that she could choose this man she was growing to love, or she could choose the man she'd loved much longer.

She lifted her chin. Her hand dropped. She tore the night robe over her head and flung it in a corner, and then dressed in the first gown at hand. Then she waited, her dreams growing as dim as the lantern.

This time she let them go.

No force on earth could have kept her from mourning their passing.

* * *

Below, Drake strode up and down in the darkness, his fist still clenched about his gift to her. His throat ached with the bellow of rage he suppressed. Damn the wench, he should tell her who was master here. He held her freedom, her horse, even her new venture, though she did not know it yet.

Why did she melt into his arms, kiss him that way, promise in action if not in word to be his, then so cruelly reject him? Pah, she was trying to drive him mad, and almost succeeding.

Drake stumbled over something, decided he'd had enough of this cursed darkness, and struck a tinder to light a lantern. He picked up the object and stared at it. Clyde's hat. He must have forgotten it. Drake checked an exquisite clock set in the belly of a sea serpent with a mermaid riding on it.

Almost ten. Clyde should have been back hours ago. *No wonder I'm so hungry.* Drake's stomach growled at that moment, adding to his irritation. Even if the authorities had stopped Clyde, they couldn't have found anything because if they had they would have been beating on his door long past. He tossed the jewel that would have purchased a small country estate on a table, glancing unseeingly at the gash in his hand.

Something was wrong. Clyde would have given them a cold supper if he'd planned to be gone so long. Drake scowled up the stairs at the quiet alcove. *Something else to lay at your door, you little vixen. If he's hurt, I shall never forgive you for distracting me.*

It was a measure of his wounded feelings that he didn't even realize how unreasonable he was. He had flung on his black leather clothes when he heard the scratching on the concealed exterior door. He hurried over to it.

"Clyde?"

The Gentle Beast

"Wilkes. Open up. I have news."

Drake rotated the pulley that raised the door, closing it just as swiftly. "Well, man?"

"Quartermain's men have him, or so I'm told by two of my sources in Whitefriars."

Drake cursed richly and long. He stuck the thin jeweled dagger in his boot, attached a brace of pistols to his shoulder, and covered them with a coarse black coat far different from his usual attire. He stuck an eye patch in his pocket and caught a fistful of cold ashes, scattering them over him.

Wilkes watched with amusement. "You should be known as Chameleon rather than Dragon. Do you need any help?"

"Only to know his location. I work best alone."

"Pity. I was about to suggest that you take your little vixen with you."

Drake whirled on Wilkes. "She is none of your concern. You may not agree with her politics, but by God you will respect her, especially in my presence. Now where is Clyde?"

Wilkes's color had gone high, but he answered calmly, "He was seen being carried into the old Red Hen Inn on Water Street." Wilkes cocked his head, obviously expecting Drake to start at the mention of one of the most notorious streets in London.

Without a visible reaction, Drake buttoned his coat. "Thanks. If I need help I shall send a message with one of your men, using the code."

"Very well. Stay safe. I need you." Wilkes melted into the night as Drake opened the door for him.

Wryly Drake watched him go. He knew Wilkes well enough by now to realize that once his usefulness was over, that spurious loyalty would evaporate. Since this opportunistic streak had led to their collusion, however, Drake could hardly condemn him for it. Especially as Drake had a glimmer of the same quality.

That quality was apparent in the steady blue gaze that lifted to the curtain. The heavy fabric quivered, as if it had just been put into place, and he knew she must have seen Wilkes come and go.

Good. Let the little witch stew in the broth of her own making. When she was properly done and tender, maybe he'd make a meal of her.

Drake's teeth gritted together as he denied the urge to go to her and whisper more tender things. He slipped outside, put the door back down, locked it, and looked up and down the deserted alley. When he was certain no one watched, he pulled off the mask, put on the eye patch, and rubbed the soot on his hands over his face. Then, swaggering like a drunkard, he turned toward Whitefriars.

Startling against the grime, his eye glowed with eagerness.

Nothing put things in perspective better than a good bout of fisticuffs. If they were lucky, he could get Clyde out with no more. If not . . .

Drake patted the pistol in his coat.

Inside, Callista slipped down the stairs. She'd seen Wilkes come, then leave as abruptly, and it made her own flight all the more imperative. She had to get out of here before Drake was caught, lest she be involved, too.

The growing justification for her flight did not make it any easier. She held her breath as she pressed the three curlicues at the same time. The panel swung open. Callista lifted her feet to walk to freedom, but somehow they dragged. At the opening she paused and looked back. From here she couldn't see the bed, which

The Gentle Beast

was just as well. But the settee where he'd kissed her, the table where they'd supped and quarreled, and the desk he wrote at were clear in the bright light he'd turned up.

Resolutely she turned back around and plunged into the dark stairwell. It clicked shut behind her.

Then the beautiful room was lonely, the treasures collected from the world over waiting to be useful again. The clock chimed midnight, the bells loud and true, but there was no one there to hear them.

Chapter Eight

Whitefriars, the most notoriously nasty, dangerous criminal haven in all of England, owed its name to a more benign influence. Centuries ago, good friars who wore white cassocks dwelled there, from whence they went to do their good deeds.

The present denizens seldom went hence; their deeds were even less often good. Most of the men and women who lived in this squalid huddle of rotting, fetid buildings were either wanted by the law, debtors escaping prison, or those wretched poor who had long ago given up hope of better lives. These latter subsisted on scraps, scrounging for coal by the Thames, or selling themselves for a meal.

Nevertheless, with all its wickedness, Whitefriars was more egalitarian than the rest of England. The great leveler here was not birth or property, but the clink of gold. Even this den of iniquity had its hierarchy, however. The lords here supped on the best china and linens—stolen; drank the best wine—smuggled; danced with the loveliest harlots—kidnapped.

Without birth or property, these criminal kings still had power aplenty. The power of life and death. With the proper bribe, they would kill anyone in any manner asked, or merely torture the victim until he wished to die. And their fiefdoms were usually more impregnable than Windsor Castle itself.

Such was the hell facing Drake as he swaggered off Fleet Street into the narrow, sewer-infested alleys. He'd thrived on the docks of Shanghai, prospered in the pirate dens of Algiers, and even survived capture by the thugs of India. Nevertheless, his confident step faltered for an instant at his first venture into White-friars. His aristocratic nose quivered at the stench that aroused too many memories he'd tried to forget. His eye darted about warily. He debated removing the eye patch, but decided his eyes were too distinctive. He didn't want to be recognized, in the unlikelihood anyone who had known his father lived here.

Still, his skin crawled with every step deeper into this festering maze. Over there a dice game was growing ugly.

In that alley a man beat a woman. On the sagging floor above to the right a drunken trull shrieked obscenities at her client, who'd apparently refused to pay.

A dog, foaming at the mouth, darted at Drake. He kicked it away with a booted foot. It flew backward, landed on its feet, and ran in the opposite direction. Nimbly Drake skirted a dice player who lurched out into the street, drawing a knife to launch himself at another gamer.

The Dragon bore onward, but it was not fear that troubled him. Only the thought of Clyde in trouble

Colleen Shannon

steeled him to this living hell he'd fought tooth and nail to escape.

Alert for danger, he still forced himself to plan a strategy. Doubtless Quartermain had chosen the most artful criminal of the lot. Wilkes had told him to look on Water Street, which was near the heart of the district, on one of the most impregnable alleys.

Drake scowled when two tough-looking men stalked toward him with what could only be described as malicious intent. Drake eased his coat back, showing the brace of pistols, and drew the knife from his boot. Without missing a step, they veered to the side, obviously seeking easier prey.

Ten minutes later, his nose told him he'd reached his destination before he saw it. The Thames here reeked. More important, it made a strategic buttress along the street, which had but one entrance. Drake's steps started to veer drunkenly as he breached the outer barrier of boxes and barrels.

Pulling a flask from his pocket, he sprinkled some rum on himself, then took a hefty swig. He felt the movement behind him and swerved abruptly in the opposite direction, reeling around to peer at the three men who confronted him. One man held a club, the other a knife, and the last a rusted but obviously serviceable pistol.

"If ye wants ta see tomorrow, ye'd best go out the ways ye come in." The tallest of the three was a burly man dressed in the finest satin and linen. Drake squinted in the dim glow cast by the soot-encrusted lanterns.

All the hair on the man's bald head had apparently migrated to his hairy wrists, which poked comically from the dirty fall of fine lace. The steady hand that held the pistol, however, was nothing to laugh at.

206

The Gentle Beast

Drake wiped his mouth on his sleeve. "Thank you, my good man, but I'm exactly where I need to be at the moment."

The cultured sound of his voice got the reaction he wanted. The three men looked at each other as if they couldn't believe such a fat pigeon had flown willingly into their nest. They gathered themselves to jump him, but Drake adroitly did what he was expert at—the unexpected.

He tossed his purse their way.

The leader caught the purse, his surprised look changing to greed. He opened the purse, counted the guineas, counted again, his eyes bugging out.

Drake set the flask away, along with his act of drunkenness. Both had served his purpose. "And there's far more where that came from—for the right business partner. Who's the master of this abominable domicile?" he asked with a smile.

The words they didn't understand, but the meaning they caught well enough. "Felix Norther. Oo's askin'?" The leader glanced at the lit window above their heads, shifted the tempting weight of gold, then reluctantly closed and pocketed the bag.

"Someone with connections that will interest him. I can show him where there's at least ten times that amount stored, and I can get him in and out without the least trouble from the law."

"All right and tight?"

Drake winked. "Tight as a virgin's tits."

This drew ribald laughter from the trio, as he'd expected. Some of their suspicion eased.

The leader's expression grew grim as he searched Drake and found the pistols. He slung them over his shoulder. "Come along then, but I warns ye—I got a pistol in yer back and the stones to weight ye with if ye tries anythin'."

"Ah, so that's why the Thames has that lovely, malodorous scent. Lead on, my good man."

Drake was marched up rotting steps to a rare mahogany door with a lion-head knocker that might have graced the finest house in Grosvenor Square. Drake squinted at it more closely. By Jove, it *had* graced the Endicott mansion.

The leader gave an odd series of knocks, which were returned. Then the door swung open to a blaze of light and glory. Drake stared, so surprised that he was only vaguely aware of the weapons leveled at him from every corner. The interior was a pleasing contrast to the ramshackle exterior. Roman statuettes and art by lesser-known but still respected English painters adorned the silk-hung walls.

Three stories soared above his head, all with balconies overhanging the central marble foyer. The open architecture of the building would make it difficult to sneak away. Drake was distracted by the opening of a door off the foyer. He glimpsed a roaring fire, a fur rug, and a naked woman, before a man in a scarlet dressing gown strode into the hall. "What's going on here, you idiot?" roared the individual who could only be Felix Norther. "Why did you bring this . . . lout into my home?"

Felix Norther was a tall, handsome man with a full head of black hair and a nose that was almost as aristocratic as Drake's. Despite his cultured words, however, his accent still hinted at his origins.

"Well, he give me this, and said he had an interestin' business deal fer ye." The leader tossed the bag of gold at his master.

Norther caught it, opened it, and counted. His scowl

Thrill to the most sensual, adventure-filled Historical Romances on the market today...

FROM  LEISURE BOOKS

As a home subscriber to Leisure Romance Book Club, you'll enjoy the best in today's BRAND-NEW Historical Romance fiction. For over twenty-five years, Leisure Books has brought you the award-winning, high-quality authors you know and love to read. Each Leisure Historical Romance will sweep you away to a world of high adventure...and intimate romance. Discover for yourself all the passion and excitement millions of readers thrill to each and every month.

Save $5.⁰⁰ Each Time You Buy!

Each month, the Leisure Romance Book Club brings you four brand-new titles from Leisure Books, America's foremost publisher of Historical Romances. EACH PACKAGE WILL SAVE YOU $5.00 FROM THE BOOKSTORE PRICE! And you'll never miss a new title with our convenient home delivery service.

Here's how we do it. Each package will carry a FREE 10-DAY EXAMINATION privilege. At the end of that time, if you decide to keep your books, simply pay the low invoice price of $16.96, no shipping or handling charges added. HOME DELIVERY IS ALWAYS FREE. With today's top Historical Romance novels selling for $5.99 and higher, our price SAVES YOU $5.00 with each shipment.

AND YOUR FIRST FOUR-BOOK SHIPMENT IS TOTALLY FREE!

IT'S A BARGAIN YOU CAN'T BEAT! A Super $21.96 Value!

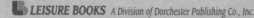 LEISURE BOOKS A Division of Dorchester Publishing Co., Inc.